Her Sister's Husband

Her Sister's Husband

Smokey Moment

Published by Smokey Moment, 2020.

This is a work of fiction. Similarities to real people, places, or events are entirely coincidental.

HER SISTER'S HUSBAND

First edition. September 4, 2020.

Copyright © 2020 Smokey Moment.

ISBN: 979-8227637017

Written by Smokey Moment.

Also by Smokey Moment

Her Sister's Husband

Table of Contents

Her Sister's Husband.. 1

Chapter One – Call Me Alexis 7

Chapter Two – The Simple Life.......................................28

Chapter Three – Penny 41

Chapter Four – Paula...55

Chapter Five – The Request...71

Chapter Six – Pitch Black..80

Chapter Seven – Attached..91

Chapter Eight – Home Bound 106

Chapter Nine – Crumbling Walls 126

Chapter Ten – Perfection 139

Chapter Eleven – The Other Misses.............................. 149

Chapter Twelve – An Unstoppable Love 157

A
Smokey Moment
Novel

SMOKEY MOMENT

WEBSITE

3

www.smokeymoment.com

Acknowledgments

I write about love because I believe in it. And I believe in all the parts of it that make one love story different from the next. Each unique. Some tragic. Others wonderful, blissful and the stuff dreams are made of. And it's in those differences, that we find ourselves. Between the pages of our own story, that we find the heart and soul of another human being.

This book is especially written for romance book lovers around the globe. A special thank you. Your cheers, constructive criticisms, commitment and support have shaped a generation of some of the best romance writers that ever existed. Thank you from the bottom of my heart!

Smokey Moment

SMOKEY MOMENT

books

STAY CONNECTED

scan the code and sign up to receive a free eBook. Get special promotional offers, chapter snippets, free book information, cover reveals, notification of new releases and so much more!

Table of Contents

Chapter One – Call Me Alexis3

Chapter Two – The Simple Life9

Chapter Three – Penny3

Chapter Four – Paula 96

Chapter Five – The Request22

Chapter Six – Pitch Black38

Chapter Seven – Attached58

Chapter Eight – Home Bound82

Chapter Nine – Crumbling Walls16

Chapter Ten – Perfection37

Chapter Eleven – The Other Misses53

Chapter Twelve – An Unstoppable Love66

Chapter One – Call Me Alexis

"Where would you like this box ma'am," the mover said to Pebbles. She gave him a look. The box was clearly marked. Pebbles, who now went by the name Alexis, was a woman on the move. She had changed her name legally, as part of her personal rebranding now that she'd made it. She pointed, as she continued talking and moving around hurriedly, totally unaware the mover was still standing in the doorway.

She unpacked the smaller boxes in the kitchen, stopping and bursting into a hearty laugh, as he stood there. He waited for the young, beautiful and well-paying customer to look up. But she was deep in conversation with someone on the phone, and the mover grew frustrated with her lack of attention to the matter at hand.

"Ma'am," he said with a sigh.

"That goes in the front room," she said, then rolled her eyes when he walked away.

She had taken the time to mark each box in big bold letters. He needed to pay attention. It took her hours to mark everything for their convenience. Besides, she didn't want to be disturbed. She was in a delightful conversation with her free-spirited and ever-present sister Penny, who was giving her the latest details of her torrid love life.

"You know you need help," she joked to her sister.

"Uh yeah! Not my fault I was blessed with all this goodness. He's just a little stalkerish. I caught him doing a drive by. Gonna have to let him go now. I do not play that shit," she said. Alexis laughed. It didn't take much for Penny to be on to the next.

"When are you going to settle down? I can't keep up."

"Never! Good pussy don't settle down! Not unless you can check all the right boxes. And he needed a lot more checks. Damn!" Penny said. Alexis shook her head. That was Penny. Her femme fatale of a sister who always somehow managed to come up with stalkers.

Not that she didn't know anything about it herself. She had one or two. But Alexis was on a mission. Her company was taking off. She had built it from scratch and she was too busy being the next "it" CEO.

"I'm coming by as soon as you get settled," Penny said. Alexis smiled. She was proud of her accomplishments. The condo was worth showing off. She couldn't wait for Penny to see it. It was a long way from their humble beginnings on Lester Avenue. Humble beginnings that made her the woman she was today.

"Mom said Paula called," Alexis said, changing the subject and bracing for the reaction. Paula was their older, long-lost sister who wasn't really lost. She just wanted nothing to do with her family, and hadn't seen her sisters in years. Penny didn't like the snub by her bougie and self- loving sister and chose to cut off contact. But Alexis, who was the peace maker of the family, just tried to get past it.

"There you go... Ruining my fucking high. Who cares? I don't! I don't care about her fake ass life. I don't care about her fake ass husband. And I certainly don't care about that fake ass money. Even her tits and ass are fake. Did you see that interview she did? It was on that podcast we used to listen to. She said they were worth a hundred million dollars. One hundred million! Please! If that's the case then why doesn't she send mom more money. Cause she wants someone to beg her for something. Get on all fours and grovel. I mean...she is obviously doing much better than you and I. Ungrateful bitch," Penny fumed.

"She's just going through something, that's all."

"Don't start defending her Pebbs," Penny replied. Alexis sighed. She wished Penny weren't so unforgiving. They were, after all, sisters.

"I'm just saying, she has issues."

"Yeah, like the fact that she doesn't want to be married to him. Discards him like a pair of old shoes. Like she did us. She ain't foolin me. That shit built on money. Plain and simple," Penny stated.

It was hard for her to feel sorry for her sister if she was truly unhappy. Paula always took things for granted. And Penny disliked the woman her sister had become. Alexis still had hope for a reunion. They needed to kiss and make up and become sisters once again. Close, as they were when they were young girls.

But life had a way of changing people. And Paula had reinvented herself. Just not in a way that was embraced by her family. And no one noticed or despised the change more than Penny.

"She doesn't love him. He's not her type. You know what I'm saying Pebbs," she said.

"Why do you say that. She does love him. She's happy. And no, I don't believe that. You have no proof."

"Yeah, well... Keep thinking that. And I have my gut! I know what it looked like," Penny said.

"Well... anyway... what you drinking? What got you high?"

"I hit Robbie's blunt. You know I don't smoke, but I couldn't resist. He brought me some food. I swear I be missing him sometimes. But we're friends. He actually makes a better friend than anything. Oh well," Penny said, reminiscing on her ex.

"Yeah...I always liked him. That's who you should have married."

"He got a little dick Pebbs. Like...Just stop! Do not fix me up or try to marry me off, cause you do *not* be paying attention. I told you that. Do you be listening. It wouldn't work! Can't eat my pussy all day long. A girl needs more than that," she said. Alexis burst into laughter. Her sister was a hot mess to say the least.

***

The women continued to talk, as Pebbles unpacked her boxes and put the items away. She had just moved from a one-bedroom luxury apartment, to a much bigger three bedroom luxurious condo.

Life had been good for Ms. Pebbles Allen who had decided to go by her middle name, Alexis. Her design company, Alexis Allen Designs, which specialized in homes and small businesses in the Atlanta area had grown considerably after she landed one of her biggest clients. A company call Dalton Industries.

Alexis started the company out of her first apartment. She ran around walking through the doors of businesses convincing them to invest in the look of their office. Soon she began working with larger companies. She had a few furniture wholesalers that she partnered with that provided her with deep discounts on select furniture lines. And with the design skills she'd acquired, she was able to design offices splendidly on a budget.

Soon after, she was earning six figures all on the heels of her drive and ambition. Word of mouth became her greatest marketing help. It wasn't long before she was earning enough money to rent space in a small building and start her company. She never looked back.

"Well anyway. How do the movers look? Anything good?" Penny asked.

"Penn...Stop! They're regular guys."

"Regular with big dicks or..." Penny said, chuckling at her candor.

"I'm not superwoman. I can't see through a pair of Levi's. But maybe," she said, as she looked around making sure none of the men were close enough to hear.

"One of them has that walk. You know," she continued, in a low voice, as she quickly glanced around. Penny laughed then quickly took on a more serious tone.

"Wait... What! I should come there now! Test out this dress I have on," Penny joked.

"No! Stay your ass at home. Don't come over here embarrassing me. I swear."

Penny was her gutsy and brave older sister. The second born of three girls and the most free speaking woman she knew. It was better that she stay put. Penny lacked the reserve that a lot of women would have around a group of strange men. She was brave and open enough to get into a conversation with the movers and possibly ask them whether or not they considered themselves well hung or not.

Her freedom had gotten them into jams in the past. But for a woman as sexually liberated as Penny was, she still enjoyed committed one on one relationships, whenever she was lucky enough to find someone to fill the shoes of all her previous lovers. Alexis had an unbreakable bond with her. They leaned on each other for everything. Their bond was more like close friends. There was just one problem. There were three Allen sisters not two. And Alexis missed Paula.

****

Alexis smiled as she unpacked more boxes. She stopped to take a moment to reflect. She had finally gotten to where she wanted to be. She had driven by that location for years, and always told herself that one day she would have enough money to move into them. It was an overwhelming triumph. One she couldn't say she was too surprised about. Once she put her mind to something, she usually achieved it.

"Here's another one. I think this is the last one," the young gentleman said, as he stared at Alexis hoping to get her number.

"Thank you," she said, as she handed him a hundred dollar tip. His warm smile was appreciated although his eyes clearly spoke of a man who wanted something else. He was cute. But Alexis was not Penny. She did not like to experiment. Dating just for the sake of dating was not her thing. But still, he was cute.

"I appreciate your crew taking care of my things," Alexis said. The man nodded then turned and walked towards the door. He looked back once. "Damn she fine," he said under his voice as he left out.

Alexis smiled. Fine she was, but *fine* didn't get her where she was. *Fine* didn't pay her way through school and *fine* never protected her from poverty during those rough adolescent and early teenage years. But fine probably did help her land Dalton Industries. The owner was still coming up with every excuse in the book to drop by her office. He was a handsome, Italian sex magnet with green eyes and dark hair but Alexis was steering clear of the married father of three. Affairs were not for her. That was her older sister Penny's thing.

A

fter a few days, Alexis was settled. She still had a few more boxes to unpack but was all but moved in. Each day ended the same. With her plopping down on her mattress and falling into a deep sleep. This evening was better. Much of what she owned was put away. The sun was no longer high in the sky and night drew near. She placed what little food she had in the refrigerator, as she heard her phone buzz. It was Penny calling to check on her. Alexis glanced at the phone as she carried the last of the boxes to her bedroom. "I'll have to call her back," she mumbled.

She had just talked to their mother. Paula had called again. Alexis was happy about the news. She hoped it meant Paula was feeling sisterly and was ready for a visit. Why else would she call back to back. It was hard to say. Paula could be unpredictable. Alexis decided not to mention the call. It wasn't worth upsetting Penny and getting her all worked up. Penny would probably show her disapproval of it. She never forgave Paula for the way she left things and the fact that she never visited or reached out. Not even on her wedding day. A move that all but severed what little bond was left.

Paula always seemed embarrassed and ashamed at her sisters' stations in life and lack of upward mobility. Part of the redesign of her image was hiding the poverty-stricken background she grew up in. Her belief that it would tarnish her reputation and keep her from the best that life had to offer, fueled her decision to avoid the family. That included everything, even weddings and funerals. Calls on holidays had become her thing until one day, even those were less frequent.

But Paula was unaware that Alexis had done well for herself. Neither sister had talked to Paula in over a year. Their mother Priscilla was the only one still receiving occasional calls. But even those calls were short and lacked any depth or deep affection. Paula always seemed to be interested in just hearing Priscilla's voice. The last time they spoke, she rushed off the phone after a few minutes to take a business call and Priscilla made every excuse for her daughter's lack of interest.

But Alexis was over family issues. She had a life to live. She was an attractive twenty seven year old and had been on her own since she was nineteen. The Allen sisters were popular all through grade school and high school. All the girls hung around them and all the boys wanted to date them. Their father, Mr. Barry Allen, ran the house like boot camp with tough rules and discipline and kept them busy with house chores and homework. His rigid ways caused friction, mostly with Penny who loved her freedom. She was boy crazy and Mr. Allen's tight rein got in the way of her young and imaginative dreams of boys and dating. Paula found creative ways around his meddling and Alexis chose to simply follow the rules.

Barry worked the night shift at a car parts manufacturing company where he'd met their mother, Priscilla Hudson. Priscilla was one of the secretaries and Mr. Allen worked the line. She was already the mother of two young girls when they met. Penny was only two years old when Priscilla became pregnant with Pebbles. The two got married when she was six months pregnant and Barry assumed the role of father to her other girls. A role Penny wasn't fond of. He doted mainly on Pebbles and Penny missed her real father.

After the girls got older and the boys started showing them attention, Barry took a more direct approach to keep the boys at bay. He came to the school to get his daughters every day, mean mugging any boy within view. But the sisters managed to evade their fathers' watchful eye and took turns sneaking out. On occasion they would let boys in their basement while their father slept. Over time resentment grew. They hated how sheltered their lives were and rebelled. But when he died suddenly, the sisters' world turned upside down when their mother fell into a deep depression.

Their mother couldn't handle the loss and was never the same, losing her mind and being put on a ton of medications just to get by. The girls were split up, with Paula going to live with her biological father and Alexis and Penny going to stay with their maternal grandmother. Paula, Penny and Pebbles had different fathers between the three of them. Barry Allen was Pebbles biological father.

"I don't understand why you never answer your phone Pebbs," Penny said, as she walked past her.

"Hello to you too. And stop calling me that. It's Alexis. Why is that so hard for you to remember," she replied, smiling at Penny. Penny was two years older than Alexis and was her polar opposite.

Alexis was more laid back and had only been in few serious relationships but Penny, who was more sexually open and free spirited, had been in many. Too many to keep up with but who was counting. Not her.

She could care less. She liked living on her own terms. She did what she wanted and tried to keep from hurting people. But sometimes she couldn't help how involved some of the men became and so she experienced more than her share of domestic problems. She had to put restraining orders on several partners in the past and had since, tried to slow her road. Her life was the life of three women rolled into one. She looked forward to her next great love affair. Not marriage. Not motherhood. For Penny, it was the love of man and woman. The bond. The courtship. The rest was for the birds.

Alexis looked her sister up and down. Penny was never one to disappoint. She wished she had half her wit and feminine prowess. It was admirable. But it wasn't for her. Yet she still admired her for all she was.

"Where you on your way to?" she asked, noticing Penny was way too overdressed for a social visit.

"Out! You should come with me. Me and Leah going to a club called *Black Bottom*," she replied.

"Black Bottom! I'm not going to no club called that. What kind of place is it?" Alexis replied.

"It's an after-hour spot. All the hotties be there. They be fine as hell. It's like a magnet for all the fine muthafuckas. What chile please! If you only knew! Come see. Plenty fun. Drinks on the house. You should come go with me. I promise you won't be disappointed. Maybe find your next dick. Come on. Get dressed," Penny said, opening Alexis' refrigerator.

"What you got to eat?" she asked.

"Damn Pen! You stay hungry. You stay overdressed. And you always going to some club to meet some loser ass guy," she chuckled as she glanced over and looked inside her fridge.

"Don't you see the meats? I have cold cuts. Turkey and Ham. You can make a sandwich," she said, as she continued cleaning and putting away her dishes. Alexis looked over and saw Penny texting and sighed.

"Move out my way. I'll make the sandwich for you," she said, opening the refrigerator and grabbing what she needed. Penny looked at her phone, chewing her gum and smiling as she watched a call from a gentleman named Laron go into voice mail.

"We should do something. I'm bored. A friend of mine keeps calling. Wants to see me. I'm thinking about meeting him out," she said, smiling at her phone as he called again.

"Who are you seeing now? I swear Pen. I can't keep up. I thought you broke up with Mark," she stated.

"I'm not seeing him. That fuckboy was a straight stalker. I had to get away from him. I've been seeing this guy I met name Tony. Girl... Damn... If I tell you about that man there I'll have to kill you.. He is hands down the best fuck ever. Big ass dick. And he knows what to do with it. I just ...Ooh lawd...Don't get me started," Penny said.

Alexis laughed. That was Penny. If one lover didn't work out, he was immediately replaced with another. Men were plentiful. But Penny was looking for love. And she would continue discarding the men until she found what she wanted. Alexis too hoped to find Mr. Right. Just not so aggressively.

"You should come. I'll help you unpack the rest tomorrow. Go get ready. You know how long you take," Penny said, looking at Alexis, hoping she agreed to go. Penny hadn't heard back from Leah and she wanted to make sure she had a hanging partner.

"If it's liquor you want, I got some of that. I've got wine and some of those coolers," she said.

"Wine! Coolers! Hell no Pebbs. I need real liquor and I need men. So do you. What has it been... like maybe a year since you fucked. You need to dust the cobwebs off," Penny joked, grinning at her sensitive baby sister. Alexis shot her a look.

"Not a year. Damn Penny. Like four months maybe. And I'm not going anywhere with you if you refuse to call me Alexis," she replied. Penny looked at her with serious eyes. She didn't understand Pebbles insistence on changing her name.

"Why would you want to go by the name *he* called you," Penny said, looking intently at her sister.

"Don't start Penn. That's all I have left of our father. The name he gave me and called me," she replied.

Penny shook her head then exhaled sharply. The origin of the name was a sore spot for their mother. But Pebbles was a daddy's girl. And she needed something to cling to. Penny didn't understand and didn't support it totally, but she loved Pebbles and would be there for her regardless.

"Momma hated making that your middle name. She said it was his mistresses name. How in the hell does a man name his child his mistress' name. Momma a good one! I would have killed him for even trying me. I'll call you that but..." Penny said, walking to the sink and placing her cup down. Alexis paused and looked at Penny. Her mood had changed.

"Why you hate him so bad? Just because he was a little strict," Alexis asked. Penny looked at her then shook her head.

"He loved another woman Alexis! Or have you forgotten that part. He was no good. And when he died momma lost it. I don't blame him for dying. I do blame him for the way he treated her before he died. And he only really ever cared about you. He wasn't my father Pebbs," Penny expressed, as she took the sandwich from her then walked into the living room.

Alexis looked off. Penny could be overly dramatic. But she wasn't a liar. It was true even if she tried to forget those days. He was her father still. And like the mounds of forgiveness she bestowed upon Paula, Pebbles forgave her father's indiscretions and was supportive to a fault. Something Penny was not. Alexis shook it off and put the bread and mayonnaise back, then finished unpacking and putting away her items.

"I'll go but only for a minute. If you have plans on being there for hours on end, then I'll drive my own car so I can leave when I want."

Clubs and after-hours spots were never Alexis' thing. She would occasionally go with her sister just to spend time with her. If she ever wanted to see her, she would have to go out because Penny went out often.

"Has mom talked to Paula?" Penny asked Alexis. Paula, the oldest sister, rarely reached out to them but if she was going to ever call either of them, it would be Alexis. Paula and Penny never got along and argued constantly.

Things came to a head when Penny, after a night of drinking, slept with Paula's boyfriend of four years. They hadn't spoken since. Penny accused Paula of doing the same thing. A terrible secret that was revealed at her engagement party. Their relationship never recovered and Penny still harbored resentment.

"I don't think so. Not lately. We should go to New York. Pop up on her," Alexis suggested.

"What! Hell no! I'm not going. She never calls and thinks she's too good, even for ma. I'm not going to see her. Not ever," Penny replied.

"That's your sister. Don't talk like that. At least call her," Alexis stated.

"Call her and say what to her bougie ass. Fuck that! If she wants to act like she doesn't exist and play us to the left, then she won't exist. I'm not kissing her ass Pebbs, I mean Alexis," she assured.

"Let's go! I do think I need that drink after all," Alexis said, as she walked toward her bedroom. She threw on a dress and heels, applied some make up and perfume and walked out the door with Penny headed for *Black Bottom*.

"How do I look? Does this dress seem too plain?" Alexis asked. The Allen sisters were always the prettiest girl around and Penny loved the attention they got, especially when they were together. Alexis had sex appeal and was never fazed by the attention of men like Penny was. She tried to avoid too much attention, but usually ended up drawing the most.

"You look stunning Alexis and you haven't even put effort in. You kill me. You look freakin gorgeous. Now stop worrying."

T

he sisters' pulled up to *Black Bottom* and tried to find a parking spot close to the door. It was busy as usual. The local cops allowed the establishment to run because the owners brother was a well-known cop.

"That dress wasn't that short when we left the house," Alexis said.

"I know tricks. You gotta learn these little tricks. You just hike it up a little and bam, instant mini," Penny said, as she giggled.

The women walked in and looked around. Alexis smiled at the bouncer as she made her way inside. Music blasted through the speakers, and the jam-packed dance floor gave the sisters dance fever. Penny snapped her fingers and swished her hips from side to side. "I want to dance. Yes! But first a drink," she said.

The club was in a rural area with no houses around and was run by a gangster name Solid. Solid looked exactly how one would imagine. He was a handsome, big, muscular, tough looking man and was nothing to play games with.

He ran Black Bottom with ease because no one fucked with him. He had a thing for Penny and even more so, Alexis, who rarely came out. Solid went way back with the Allen sisters and used to date Paula first before dating Penny when Paula went away to college. He had hoped to get acquainted with Alexis next.

"What's up," Penny shouted, trying to talk over the music to Solid, as she grinned and flirted with him. Alexis smiled and looked around as Penny talked and with him. A young lady walked up to Penny and the two kissed each other on the cheek before Penny ordered two shots of tequila for herself and her sister. Alexis noticed a guy she thought she knew and turned to her sister. "I'll be back. I think that's Ralph," she said, walking in the direction of the pool tables.

"I thought that was you," Alexis said, as she approached. Alexis hugged Ralph then pushed away after the hug went a little longer than she wanted.

"Damn girl! You ain't changed one bit. Still fine as fuck," he said, as he looked her up and down.

Alexis smiled and looked around slowly, trying to see if there was anyone else there she recognized. Ralph always had a crush on the sisters, but no one could get past their over bearing father. So he, like many others, could only dream. Ralph asked her if she was drinking and she told him she liked tequila shots.

"I'll be right back my love," Ralph said, as he walked away to get her a shot. Alexis stood next to his buddy, who was in a coma like stare that was making her uncomfortable. She looked at him several times all while praying Ralph returned sooner that later.

The man was being weird. His stare was intense and she was ready to remove herself from his path. Alexis noticed his other buddies, as they whispered in each other's ear. *What the fuck. Am I the only woman here,* she thought, as she looked towards the bar. Ralph was deep in conversation with the bartender and she was still counting the minutes until his return. His, was the only face she knew.

"Here you go," he said, as he handed her the shot. His friends seemed to suddenly lose interest. Ralph was a nice guy only to women. The men knew not to disrespect him. He could be violent. Something Alexis knew nothing about. She only knew him in a sense of knowing his face. Ralph was dirty. The type of guy a woman needed to keep far from.

"So, tell me what you been up to," he asked. It wasn't long before the DJ switched to Grand Master Flash's, *The Message,* and Alexis wanted to dance.

"You want another shot," Ralph asked.

Alexis shook her head no. She knew her limit. Two shots were all she could do. Any more than that, and Ralph may be able to get her on her back. He was, after all, sexy as hell.

Penny continued talking with Solid as he pulled on her, kissing her neck and grabbing her ass. She constantly looked over in Alexis' direction to keep an eye on her. She knew her sister didn't handle liquor well and would turn into a free spirited sex pot under the influence. Penny didn't need liquor. She was extremely sexual, naturally, but Alexis was more reserved, except for when she drank. Penny was a lot more street savvy than Pebbles and knew that hang outs like Black Bottom was nowhere to be drunk or zoned out.

After a few minutes of laughing and talking Alexis grabbed Ralph's hand and walked to the dance floor.

"Come on let's dance," she said, as she looked back at him. Ralph licked his lips. She was sexy. He wanted to dance. It would give him chance to get closer. Perhaps touch. Maybe kiss. Women got frisky when a drink was in them. And Ralph gave an extra push. He added a little something to help loosen her right up. A cocktail his boys liked to call *pop tart*.

As the two danced, Pebbles started to feel strange and became dizzy. She tripped over her own feet, as her eyes lowered. The room felt as if it was spinning and she felt herself losing control of her body or her movements. Ralph looked around, then took her by the hand and walked towards the back of the bar. Penny looked around and suddenly panicked when she didn't see Alexis. She walked over to where she'd last seen her.

"Where'd she go?" Penny shouted at one of the guys standing near the pool table.

"I don't know. I think that way," he said, pointing towards the back of the club. Penny walked up to Solid. He sensed something was up and started towards her.

"What's wrong?" he asked.

"Can you help me find Pebbles," Penny said, as she frantically scanned the crowd. He could see the panicked looked on her face. Solid looked around and summoned a few of his buddies and told them to locate Penny's sister. They all knew the Allen girls and so they knew who they were looking for.

Penny walked in the direction of the back where the bathrooms were. Something told her Alexis was inside. There was nothing towards the back but bathrooms and Alexis never went to the bathroom alone. She always came to find her so they could go together. It was something they just did. And it didn't make sense she would start doing something in a new club she had never been in before.

Penny walked right into the men's bathroom. She stopped and gasped. "You fucking rapist. Piece of shit ass bastard! What the hell are you doing with her" she said, as she walked over to them. Ralph had his hand up Alexis' dress as she was holding onto him and looking slightly dazed.

"You asshole! What's wrong with her? Pebbs...Pebbs," she said, holding her sisters face as she stared into her droopy eyes. Alexis nodded and dropped her head, and Penny began to hit Ralph repeatedly in the top of his head. The commotion caught Solid's attention. He ran in.

"Man! What the fuck. I don't play this shit at my club. And you fucking with my girl's sister?" Solid said, as he looked at Alexis then at Penny.

"He had his hand up her dress. This muthafucka on some rape shit. She not acting like herself," Penny stated.

"What did you give her?" Penny yelled, as she held Alexis' head up. "Pebbs? Pebbs? Do you hear me. Say something" she said, as she shook her. Alexis mumbled incoherently as she dropped her head one more. Penny became more enraged. And Solid took control of the scene.

"Take her and go," he said.

Penny held Alexis up and slowly made her way to the door. She called her sisters name repeatedly, worried Alexis may pass out or have a bad reaction. Alexis stumbled, but was able to walk with Penny. She seemed intoxicated, but was still somewhat alert. Penny looked back at Ralph with an intense glare.

"You fucked with the wrong one," she said, as she opened the bathroom door.

The next morning, Alexis woke up and saw Penny asleep next to her, in her bed. She held her head as it pounded from a massive headache and looked over at her clock.

"Damn! What happened?" Alexis said. Penny woke up and looked her over.

"What the fuck Alexis. You scared the shit out of me. That muthafucka put something in your drink last night. Solid whupped his ass too," she said, gleaming with pride that they had the protection. He didn't go to bat for all women. Not himself. He would just order that the man be removed and the woman be given aid.

But he physically reacted. A plus in Penny's book. She would need to give him something wonderful as a thank you. He liked her and this endeared him to her. He wanted her back. And now, he may just be able to have her.

Alexis tried to sit up and was looking around and holding her head. "Wait. Let me get you some water. You gotta start flushing that shit out of your system," Penny said, as she kicked the covers off.

She got up, went into the kitchen and grabbed a bottle of Fiji water and then went into the bathroom and grabbed two Tylenol from the bathroom cabinet.

"Here you go," Penny said, handing her sister the pills.

"Shit! I had a meeting today."

"Yeah your secretary called. I told her to cancel that. I told her you weren't feeling too good."

"No, no, no. She can't cancel that. It took me months to get that client." Alexis blurted then took a sip of her water. She reached for her cell phone and called her secretary Sara.

"Hey it's me. What happened with the executives I was supposed to meet with today? Did you cancel already?" she asked. Sara told her that she left a voice message with the CEO and never heard back.

"Ok. I need you to call him back and tell him I can still meet with him. Tell him the first drafts are ready for him to go over," she urged. Sick or not, Alexis was a trooper and she wanted to land this account. Her company was still in its infancy and she could not continue to ride off the success of her last large client. She needed to land more clients. "Ok. I'll call them back," Sara stated.

Penny kissed her sister goodbye. She was surprised at how good Alexis looked given the fact that she was drugged the night before.

"He must not have given you a lot. There's no way your ass would be able to function the next day. I wonder what he put in your drink? He was all down your panties too. Do you remember any of it?" she said, as she looked at her sister. Alexis shrugged her shoulders.

"I don't remember. My head was killing me though. I don't feel one hundred, but I'm good enough to go in and go over this stuff. I'm coming right back home after this," Alexis assured.

Penny left her sister's new apartment, once she saw there were no lasting effects from the drug. Alexis walked to the window and watched her drive off then jumped in the shower and got dressed. Deep down she was angry at her sister. She hated those types of places and wished she hadn't gone, but she went there to watch Penny not the other way around.

She was not new to the club scene. Women got drugged and raped all the time. She hated she let her guard down. She wasn't as street wise as her sisters Paula and Penny, but she could hold her own. Or at least she thought so. It was a tough lesson learned. The truth was out of the three sisters, she was the homebody. The one who excelled in school. And the one least likely to run the streets.

The streets can't get you if you ain't out there running around in it, she thought. It was Penny who was always getting into trouble, and Alexis worried about her. Penny herself had been roofied at least twice in her adult life. But Penny caught on quick after the last time and wised up real fast.

Chapter Two – The Simple Life

"Are they here yet?" Alexis said, rushing through the door of her office.

"Not yet. I got you all set up in your conference room," Sara replied.

Alexis walked straight to her office and sat her things down before going into the conference room. She laid out the plans floor by floor and made sure she had the revised list of furniture manufacturers who would be supplying the furniture. Alexis looked up when she heard a light tap on the door. It was her top salesman and ex-lover Delano Ross.

"Hey," he said, staring at her. Delano had helped her land the account and was still hopelessly in love with her.

"Hey Delano. Are you sitting in on this one?"

She knew he wanted to. He was jealous of any competition and Mr. Lawrence Caldwell, the CEO of *Twin Peaks Technologies* was definitely someone to fear. Tall dark and handsome barely described him and it was obvious when Delano and Alexis first went to Twin Peaks, that he had his eyes on Alexis.

"Yeah. I planned on it. I'll grab my things," he said.

Alexis shook her head. She knew exactly why he would be sitting in on this meeting. Delano was not to be underestimated. He still loved her and stayed close to her in an effort to ward off any potential suitors.

But Delano was his own worst enemy when it came to her. She would have stayed with him if he wasn't so possessive. He was gifted. He was talented and smart. And he helped Alexis build the company to the powerhouse it was. He was an invaluable asset to her. But he had let his feeling for her cloud his judgement and affect his work at times.

Alexis had a thing for him but he had gotten so consumed with her that she started backing off, eventually pulling away completely.

"Ms. Allen, your ten o'clock appointment is here," Sara announced through the phone paging system.

"Thanks Sara. Send them right in and tell Delano they're here."

Alexis stood up and walked to the door and smiled as two gentlemen came in. "Well hello Ms. Allen," the owner of Twin Peaks said, shaking her hand and smiling. Alexis shook his hand and the hand of one of his managers he bought along.

"Hi. Mr. Caldwell. I have all the finished plans laid out. We can go through everything area by area and make any adjustments that you need," she said, feeling a little uncomfortable by the way he was gazing into her eyes. His stare lasted so long that she looked away hoping that would end it.

"Sorry I'm late," Delano said, as he walked in. He walked over to Mr. Caldwell and shook his hand and then shook his managers hand. The four met for almost two hours, going over the plans and making all the adjustments before a completed draft could be produced. He handed Alexis a deposit check and shook her hand as he left, looking back at her when he walked out her office door.

"He likes you," Delano said.

"No, not like that."

She knew the man did, but she would deny it until the cows came home. She didn't need any problems out of Delano.

Alexis went home early after her meeting still feeling the effects of the tainted drink from the night before. She walked through her door, removed her white silk blouse, navy pencil skirt and Manolo heels and plopped down on her bed. She rolled over and put her hands on her head. She was beginning to feel the return of the headache she felt earlier. *I need something now before this headache kicks in*, she thought.

Alexis walked to her cabinet and grabbed the Tylenol. She took two pills and went right back into her bedroom. The pounding was coming on strong. She hoped the pills would kick in. She laid on her bed, turned her tv on and began flipping through her Facebook and Instagram accounts while she watched her favorite soaps. She closed her eyes for relief and had started to drift off when she heard a knock at her door.

Damn Penny. Go home, she thought, as she made her way to her door. Penny was always popping up on her now that she was only about a ten-minute drive down New Hope Rd.

"Who is it?" she said, peeking out of her peep hole. *Dammit! What is he doing here*, she thought, at the sight of Delano standing on the other side of the door. Alexis opened the door. Her stern face and disappointed look, was all she could do to keep from verbally reprimanding him. Delano was easily affected by her and she needed him mentally together for his meeting the next morning. But he was pushing his luck. He was trying to force her hand. He wanted to rekindle an affair that ended too soon for him. He wasn't over her.

"What are you doing here," she said. Delano looked at her and walked right past her, looking around her condo.

"I was wondering why you left so soon. You left right after he did," he said. Alexis couldn't believe him. *Did he just come to my condo to check up on me?*

"Look Delano. It's none of your business what I do. We're not together anymore. Stop acting like we are," she said, as she turned and went into her kitchen. Her condo had a nice open floor plan. The kitchen opened up to the living room with no walls surrounding it. Her kitchen was all stainless steel and oak wood, with designer knobs and glass cabinet doors. It was exquisite and she loved being home. She had designed it to her liking so she could always look around and see what she had accomplished.

"You want something to drink," she asked.

"Yeah anything," he said, as he sat down on her tall kitchen island chair.

Alexis poured him a glass of homemade fresh squeezed lemonade and walked back to her bedroom to retrieve her phone. As she looked at her texts and missed calls, Delano approached her from behind.

"No! Go back in the front," she said, trying to hide the fact that she was turned on by him.

"Come on Alexis," Delano said kissing on her neck. Alexis closed her eyes. She hadn't had sex in a while and the last time she did, it was with him. She needed this.

"You know I love you woman. Stop pushing me away," he said, as he softly rubbed her breast. Delano raised up her shirt exposing her red lace Victoria secret bra. He loved her underwear, when she actually wore them. Alexis did too, and purchased only lace and satin undergarments and Delano always thought she wore it especially for him.

Delano turned her around and dove his tongue in her mouth. He was a champion kisser, with just the right amount of tongue and nothing extra. Alexis moaned. A signal he used to help himself to her perky and small, but nice sized breast. He loved her body. Alexis used to take walks. Her body showed the fact that she invested in her looks. And Delano was obsessed. He wanted her back. This time for keeps.

Alexis moaned as he sucked her nipples gently and kissed them. He stepped back and removed his shirt exposing his well-toned, muscular arms. He left his wife beater then unbuttoned his pants, as Alexis completely removed her blouse then her skirt.

"Where's your panties Alexis? Were you at work with no panties on?" he asked, his thick eyebrow raised slightly. He remembered that was something she used to do on occasion, but he always assumed she was doing that for him. They had broken up, so who was she doing it for now.

"I took them off as soon as I got here. You know I don't like panties. I barely like bras. I only wear them because my momma told me my titties would sag if I didn't keep one on."

Alexis walked seductively to the bed. She would allow him to have her. The thought of going another month without intimacy bothered her. She was in her prime. Her body craved a man's more than she liked to admit. And Delano was her best choice. There was no one else. Not that she wanted anyone. Delano was the closest thing to a relationship she had. It helped that he had nine inches for her to consume. And she would. She was horny.

Alexis laid on the bed. Delano took in the beautiful sight. She smiled then began to tease him slightly. Delano smirked seductively as he watched her touch herself. He grabbed his now rock hard erection and stroked himself then climbed in and got between her legs. He was anxious to be inside her.

She wanted him but not in the seething lustful way she once did. She used to drool over him. There was a time when entry into the bed would have her flipping around and down on him, taking him deep inside her warm mouth. This time was different. She wanted straight sex. No kinky preliminaries. But she would give him exactly what he wanted because Delano was still sexy and easy to devour. His penis with its perfect head that towered over his shaft like a ripe mushroom looked delectable.

"Stop playing with him and give it to me," she said in a whisper. Delano smiled and laid on her, then kissed her gently, taking his time as he watched her facial expression. Alexis immediately wrapped her legs around his waist, pulling him inside of her. She wanted no foreplay. She wanted him to fuck her and restart her fires that were all but dimmed from months of no sex. He was packing and he was well aware of what he did to a woman. But he wanted Alexis in a different way. The sex was good but they made a great team. But he wasn't stupid. Until she opened her heart again, he would take her pussy and serve it correctly with his long thick cock.

He pushed his tongue inside her mouth and pulled her hips close to him, slowly entering her. Alexis opened her eyes and looked down. It felt like he had grown. It seemed massive.

"Ahhh...Damn Delano! What the fuck. You bigger," she said, smiling at him.

"No! You just forgot. But I'm getting ready to remind you," he said, as he kissed her forcefully. Passionately. He pushed in deeper, and without warning grabbed her legs, cupped her ass and rammed her mercilessly.

"Delannno," she moaned, as he pounded. He slowed his strokes and took a moment to nibble her breast, taking small sucks of her perky nipples. "Ahhh. Uhmmm," she purred. He held her ass in his hands squeezing them with his large capable hands. Alexis had bit off more than she could chew. Delano missed her and it was apparent by his consistent and unrelenting strokes. He kissed her intensely. He was passionate. He was sensual.

"Open your mouth," he said looking deeply in her eyes. Alexis looked at his lips then opened her mouth and stuck out her tongue. Delano put his mouth over hers and sucked her tongue then nibbled her bottom lip. An act that had him ready to cum. She was wetter. He imagined she had already came once. He tucked his head inside her neck, raised her hips slightly, and pounded her with thrusts that would break a weaker bed. Alexis moaned loudly as her headboard slammed against the wall.

"Dellannooo," she begged, hoping he would continue his pounding. She had one more orgasm to release. It was on the edge of her insides waiting to burst and release her love juices. "Delano yes. Yes. Oh," she moaned, as he thrusted in and out. Soon his movement slowed and he yelped then jerked violently, pulling her waist up as he came inside her. Alexis could feel the sensation of his warm. She arched her back and dipped her head as he continued to shake.

"Ahh. Ahh. Shhitt," he said, his head still buried in her neck. Delano collapsed on her, holding her tight. He kissed her softly as he laid on her. Alexis closed her eyes. It was exhaustive. Her breaths were still heavy. Labored. Delano never disappointed in matters of lovemaking. Her orgasms would hold her over for a few months at least. She thought about it. He would want to talk about getting back together again. It was their main topic outside of their clients. There was work. And then there was the fact that they weren't a couple. Delano didn't move. He liked to sleep in her pussy. She would let him. He deserved as much.

Alexis woke up with Delano half on her. She tried to ease from under him but he opened his eyes then grabbed her by the hip. "Wait!" she said. It was too late. He was hard and back inside her. "No! I'm not done," he said, as he pushed his nine inches back inside again. Delano fucked her fervently, determined to get her back. He wanted her hooked on him and desiring him the way she used to. He knew he'd messed up with her with his overly aggressive stalking behavior but he also knew that at one time she loved him.

"I want you back Lex," he whispered in her ear. She moaned and clawed his back, calling his name but never responded to what he said. "You hear me," he said. "Just fuck me Delano," she managed to say as she moaned, moving her hips against him increasing the speed. It wasn't long before her sensitive vagina was once again delivering a rush of wetness on him as he stroked her with powerful thrust.

Delano was not ready to come and so he grabbed her legs and raised them higher, continuing to pound her pussy but he too was sensitive and was unable to fuck her past a few minutes. He jerked again, shooting out into her once more, as his body gave in to their intense love making session. Delano rolled off of her and held his cock, falling asleep quickly. Alexis looked over at him then eased out of bed.

Alexis left Delano sleep in her bead as she walked to the kitchen, phone in hand, to grab a snack. She sat her phone down on her table and looked through her freezer and pulled out a Swanson tv dinner. She heard her phone buzzing and saw Penny was calling.

"Hey," she answered.

"What's up girlie. What you doing," Penny said.

"Nothing. Delano here," she whispered.

"Oh shit! Yo ass finally got some dick. I'm so proud of you," Penny replied.

"Shut up Pen. He showed up on me. I let his ass in cause I needed it. He's not spending the night though. No. I'm not letting him suck me back in," she stated.

"You crazy. That man is fine as wine. I wouldn't give a fuck what he did in the past. He just in love girl. Men get stupid like that when they in love. Just like woman can get. Couldn't be me. I never would have left his ass," Penny assured.

"Yes you would have Pen cause yo ass wont date a man past three months. It's like you have an internal clock that says times up," she said, as the two laughed.

"Besides, I never said I didn't love him. I just don't want what he wants. He's not my soul mate. We're just passionate together and the sex is good but I'm looking for something more," she stated.

As the two continued to talk, Alexis looked toward the window and saw his reflection in the window and turned around. She could tell by the look on his face that he'd heard everything she said. "Pen, I gotta call you back," she said, as she hung up abruptly.

She stood there staring at him as he stared back. She felt embarrassed and awkward as she struggled to say anything to him, that would erase what he had just heard. She would never have talked to him like that. It was a sister thing and he wasn't supposed to hear any of it, even though it was exactly how she felt.

"So, I'm nothing but some dick to you?" Delano asked, staring her directly in her eyes and not flinching. He didn't even appear to blink.

"I didn't mean it like that," she replied, mortified that he'd heard her.

"Well how did you mean it," he said, shaking his head slowly from the hurt and disbelief. All the months he tried in vain to win her back and all she thought of him was a dick to get off on, nothing more.

"No... I just..." she paused, tearing up from the shame of not telling him how she felt a long time ago. Instead, she strung him along and now, she had no words to ease the moment.

Delano walked closer to her. "Tell me something Alexis. What have we been doing the whole time? You never cared about me? You never took me seriously? Why?" he asked.

"I don't know. When we met I was just breaking up with Byron. I wasn't really ready for anything serious and I told you that. I'm sorry," Alexis replied looking down, too embarrassed to look him in the face.

"Wow! Ok Alexis. I'll see you at the office tomorrow," Delano said, as he walked towards her front door and left, looking back at her before closing her door. Alexis grabbed her phone and called Penny back.

"Damn Pen he heard me. He was standing right behind me when we were talking," she said, looking out her window, watching as he got in his car.

"Well, at least he knows now. Do you want him totally out of your life or what?" she asked. "I didn't. He's ok. He just can get possessive but I know he cares about me. I didn't mean for it to go down like this," Penny replied.

"Hey ma," Alexis said as she walked in. Priscilla had just cooked a lasagna and was happy to see her youngest daughter. "Hi. You hungry. I just made your favorite," she said. "You know I do. You got it smelling good in here. You seen Penny today," she asked.

"Not yet. She called though," she replied. Alexis sat down and got comfortable. She picked up her mother's remote and began flipping through the channels. Priscilla made her a plate and brought it over.

"Thanks ma," she said, as she ate and checked her texts. She heard a car door close and looked out the window. "Here she is now ma," she said, getting up to open the door for Penny.

"Hey," Penny said, smiling as she kissed Alexis on the cheek. "Hey ma," she said kissing her mother as well.

"What's in the bag?" Alexis asked.

"I got ma some groceries. Just some basic things," Penny said, sitting the bag on the kitchen counter. She turned to her sister. She had an earful to tell Alexis but didn't want to talk in front of their mother. Alexis saw the look in her sister's eye. The women grinned. They had a pact. No secrets revealed in front of their bougie, judgmental mother.

"So what's up. Want to go with me to this all white party?" Penny asked, as she sat down at the table. Priscilla sat a plate of lasagna in front of her and she started to eat as the two talked about their day.

"No! No more parties. Besides... I have to meet with my client soon. I was supposed to be off today but he's ready to move forward so I have to go get the revised plans," Alexis stated. "Want to go shopping after you leave there? I can go with you and then we can go," Penny suggested. "Ok."

Penny and Alexis got in her Audi SUV and headed to Twin Peaks. Along the way, they stopped at Alexis' design firm and Alexis ran in to grab what Mr. Caldwell had faxed over.

"You going there alone?" Delano said walking up on Alexis.

"Yes I am. I only need to see the changes and sign it and get his signature on it," she replied.

"I should go with you Alexis," he replied, looking at her unable to hide his jealousy.

"Delano. I'm good. Besides Penny going with me. She's out in the car," she stated as she continued going through the document.

Delano walked away and went out to her car as she stood there shaking her head. When she came out he looked at her and then walked back in the office. "Ok. What the hell is he going through now," she asked. Penny smiled.

"He thinks you're in imminent danger," she said, laughing.

"I'm not dealing with him. Not today," she said, as they pulled off.

"He's going to blow this deal for me. He's been acting jealous and if my client picks up on it, he could take his business elsewhere. I need this. This is more money than the Dalton Industries deal," she said, sounding worried.

"Don't worry. You got this," Penny said, putting on her sun glasses and getting comfortable.

Alexis pulled up to Twin Peaks and her and Penny went in. Penny sat down near the reception area while Alexis walked over and spoke with the receptionist. The receptionist took her straight back to Mr. Caldwell's office.

"Hi, Mr. Caldwell," she said shaking his hand. His secretary left out shutting his door behind her and Alexis sat down and began showing him the changes. She was thrown off by his demeanor and lack of attention to the changes. He stared at her and smiled as she went area to area, showing him what she had noted and initialed.

Alexis finally looked up and stopped. "Is something wrong," she said.

"No. You're beautiful and I like to watch you talk. I love your lips," he said, grinning at her and hoping she flirted back with him.

"Mr. Caldwell. I appreciate the compliment but we have to get through this if I am to meet your deadline," she stressed. "I trust your changes. I don't want to go through the changes. I want to kiss you," he replied. Alexis stood up.

"Maybe I should come back at another time," she said.

"I already gave you the account. There's more if you let me see you," he replied as he got up from his desk and walked toward her. He got in her face and Alexis backed away as she teared up. She didn't want to lose the account but she wasn't about to let him touch her either.

"No. I have to go," she said as she left, with watery eyes, upset at his strong come on.

"What's wrong," Penny said as Alexis approached quickly. "Nothing! Let's just get out of here. He's an asshole. He tried to come on to me! I left without his signature. I probably just lost this account. Let's just go," she said walking out the door. Alexis couldn't wait to get to the car. Her hasty bolt out the door and towards the parking lot distracted her from the obvious.

She kept her eyes on the ground. This was her life. Male clients who always wanted much more. Her beauty and magnificent body were but a part of her. She took her business serious. He was not welcome to mix business with pleasure. She wanted the account still but it was impossible to talk to him when he was so unfocused.

Alexis glanced back after she noticed she could not hear Penny walking behind her. "What! Where did she go?" she mumbled, as she walked back to the building. She entered and looked around. The secretary saw the perplexed look on her face and waved her over.

"If you're looking for that woman, she's in with Mr. Caldwell," the receptionist said. Alexis chuckled then looked off. Her sister was unpredictable and a handful. She wouldn't be surprised if Penny was in his face ready to slap him for being a jerk. Alexis sat down and waited on Penny. She wasn't sure what was going on although she suspected foul play. Penny was capable of just about anything and so she would have to wait and see what she had done this time.

After several minutes Penny emerged smiling, with papers in her hand. "Here. They're signed. Can we go now?" she said. Alexis looked dumbfounded, following her gutsy and free-spirited sister out of the building. "What in the world! What happened Pen?" she said, looking perplexed.

"Nothing! Flirted a little. He's fine so, that part was easy. Told him I knew his wife. Told him he was sexy and his wife didn't have to hear from me or see my face. He signed it. Apologized for coming on so strong. Said he just finds you irresistible then told me he wanted me. I told him maybe... If he behaves," she said, as she put her sun glasses back on and got comfortable, again.

"You are something else," Alexis said, as they walked to the car. Penny sat in the passenger seat beaming. She had done a good deed. Alexis could continue with her business agreement. She was sure Mr. Caldwell got nervous at the mention of his wife. And she was sure he knew better than to try anything dirty because of an inability to screw a woman he was supposed to be doing business with.

Even still, he was cute and she liked how she'd handled him. In a different life she would have gave more of an invitation. She liked older men. Especially older successful men. But he had hurt Alexis' feelings so the flirt was nothing more. She didn't take kindly to people upsetting her family, especially Alexis.

Chapter Three – Penny

P

enny's morning started out hectic as she woke up late then scrambled to get to work on time. "Excuse me. Excuse me," Penny said, as she rushed past the crowd to get to the elevators. She was carrying coffee in one hand, her purse in another while trying to hold a large file under her arms and doing a bad job. Before she could reach the elevators, the files fell from her arms and onto the floor, landing all around her. "Shit," she said, as she tried holding her purse under her arm while she tried picking them up with one hand. She refused to sit the coffee down. She needed it.

As she struggled to gather the papers, someone kneeled down to assist her and she looked up briefly to thank them. Her mouth almost dropped as she looked into the eyes of the most handsome man she had seen in a minute and she'd seen some. "You got too much in your hand beautiful," he said, flashing a sexy smile as he grabbed the papers. Penny smiled back at him and stared at the handsome, brown skinned, athletically built man in his Ralph Lauren Suit and smelling of Gucci's *Guilty* cologne.

The two could barely pick the papers up from staring at one another. She had never seen him in the building before. It was a tall building filled with many different tenants and Penny had been working at TNT Investments as a secretary for some time. She wouldn't have forgotten such a beautiful specimen if she had seen him before.

"Thank you so much," she said, as she finished grabbing what she could. They stood up and he handed her the rest of the papers and smiled as he walked away. Penny watched as he went to the revolving exit doors and left the building. *Damn! Who was that,* she thought, as she continued onto the elevator.

"Penny your late. Tom needed those documents like an hour ago. And why are they all out of order. Oh my God Penny. We have to get these in order before his client gets here," Mrs. Taubman stated. She was the office manager and she was fond of Penny but was growing tired of Penny's nonchalant attitude and lack of commitment to her job.

She was late every other day. She walked in dressed as though she were at a club instead of a multi million dollar establishment and she missed deadlines on important things often. But when you're providing the owner with some of the best head he's ever had, you get away with that type of behavior. If only Mrs. Taubman knew, which she didn't. She was clueless as far as Penny was concerned. Penny knew to play her a certain way in order to avoid causing jealousy or resentment. "Sorry Janice. I'll have it right in no time," she replied.

Janice walked away toward her office as Penny started placing the papers in numerical order. "Hey Penny. You got the documents I need to review," Tom said, flashing his perfect smile. He was a fifty five year old, handsome white man, with dark hair and blue eyes. He hired Penny on the spot when she walked in six years ago looking for a job. He couldn't help himself.

She was the prettiest, sexiest and sweetest secretary he had ever laid eyes on. Two days later she was at his apartment on her hand and knees moaning and calling his name and the two had carried on ever since. Tom was married but separated at the time but had since, gotten back together with his estranged wife. His wife had been to the office many times and always suspected that her husband was fooling around with the sexy and beautiful secretary but was powerless to do anything.

Tom always did what he wanted, when he wanted throughout their entire marriage and if she wanted to stay relevant and in control of his money, she would have to turn a blind eye. Tom was generous with his wife and that was all she really cared about. He was generous with Penny too.

She was driving a brand new Lincoln SUV courtesy of his generosity. He was in lust with the light brown skinned, shapely vixen who dyed her short, naturally curly hair blonde and wore hazel colored contacts over her naturally brown eyes. Penny, as all her sisters, had pretty wavy hair, but Penny kept hers chopped off. She was sexy enough to get away with hair so short, she didn't need to comb it. She woke up every morning, washed it as she showered, put water and oil moisturizer in it and that was it. She perfected applying her makeup and never left the house without it.

"Sorry Tom. I dropped the papers. So, give me a moment to get them in order," she said, looking at him and giving him "the look." The look that meant; *I'm the pussy so don't fuck with me right now. I'll get this shit together but don't pressure me or you won't be getting shit tonight.*

Tom walked away and headed to his office. Penny heard her phone buzzing and looked at it. It was Alexis. "Hey girl," she said, as she talked and continued organizing the papers.

"Hey. Want to meet for lunch?" Alexis asked.

"Yeah. I can go around one. I'm sort of busy right now. I'll call you back in a few," Penny replied. The two talked for a moment before hanging up. Penny continued until she got the last paper in place then attached a clip to the pile.

Penny grabbed the file and walked into Tom's office. "Ok. They're in order," she said placing the papers on his desk.

"So am I seeing you tonight," Tom asked, grinning like a school aged boy.

"Yes Tom. Just call when you're on your way to make sure I'm there," she replied.

"Where you going Penny?" he asked, sounding like a husband, instead of the part time lover that he was.

"Out with Alexis. Just call me. I'll be home by eleven," she said.

Penny left out of his office and went back to the front desk looking straight ahead as she walked past some of the clerks and salespeople.

Mrs. Taubman was clueless but many of them weren't. They had peeped, a long time ago, what was up between her and Tom. It was office gossip that Mrs. Taubman wasn't privy to because she kept her distance and stayed in her office a lot. Many of Penny's co-workers were either jealous of her, loathed her or wanted to fuck her. She kept to herself and fed off of their resentment towards her by behaving and dressing in an even more provocative way as a personal *fuck you* to them.

She had just one friend in the whole office, Leah. Her and Leah were close and hung out and shopped together. And no matter how her other coworkers felt about her, not one of them could say that she wasn't smart and able to hold her own at TNT. Penny had attended college but never finished but it wasn't from lack of brains. She was just too much of a busy body to stand still long enough to complete anything including her personal relationships.

She was always moving from one man to another. One place to another. Her job at *TNT* was the most committed thing she had ever done. She was there six years and counting and everyone who knew her never thought they'd live to see the day that she committed to anything. That was her whole reason for never marrying or not having children. She was a true, die hard, commitment phobe.

"Hey girl," Leah said, as she approached. It was getting close to one o'clock and Penny was preparing for her lunch date with her sister.

"Hey Leah. I gotta meet Pebbles for lunch at *The Eatery*. I'm leaving soon. Want me to grab you a sandwich?" she asked.

"No. I'm good. How Pebbles been? I haven't seen her in a minute. She still with that fine ass guy?" Leah asked.

"No. You talking about Delano. Naw. She said she not feelin him. Which is crazy to me cause she like the dick. You know how she is. She wants to be in love. She doesn't like to kick it," she said, as she grabbed her purse.

"Tell her I said hi. We should all go out this weekend," Leah said, as Penny walked towards the glass exit door.

"I'll ask her."

"Hey sis," she said, kissing Alexis on the cheek.

"Hey. I'm starved," Alexis said, looking around. Penny looked down at her phone then sent a text. Alexis looked back at her sister and smiled lovingly. Penny was always texting. Always talking. She loved her sister. And deep down she envied her sister's ability to do her and not explain herself or feel any other way. Penny had always been Penny. Never changing to suit anyone's desires but her own. It was admirable.

The two were escorted to their table at the posh, small restaurant that specialized in exquisite, one of a kind lunches that were the talk of the Atlanta. Their chef was world renowned and he and a partner started *The Eatery* just a year ago and it had quickly become a popular spot for the busy, on the go Atlanta businessmen and women. "How you feel? You still upset about Delano," Penny asked, getting right to the point. She could tell that something was on her sister's mind and figured that was it.

"He's still upset. Giving me the silent treatment and avoiding me at the office. He still pulls his end and does his job so I can't say anything. I should have never started with him. He doesn't deserve his feelings hurt but I can't be with him. We're not compatible. He's not romantic. He doesn't make me feel the way I want a man to make me feel. I can't explain it. But the crazy part is, he thinks he does. If you were to ask him, he would swear up and down that he gives his all and is open but he's not. I don't know... But that's not why I wanted to meet with you for lunch. Paula called me. She left me a message to call her but then when I did, she didn't answer. I've called her four times and she still hasn't picked up or called me back. I wonder what's going on with her," Alexis said, as she looked off into the lunch crowd.

"Nothing. She doesn't want shit. Don't call her. Nobody got time for her. She always wants to call when she's in trouble. I bet you she's in some type of trouble. She knows not to call me with that bullshit. If she can't call any other time, don't call when you in trouble," Penny stated.

"Don't say that. You know you don't feel like that. Why you always talking like you hate her. Stop it," Alexis pleaded.

Penny rolled her eyes and looked away. The sisters talked through their lunch until it was time to get back to their offices. Alexis paid the tab and the two stood up and kissed each other on the cheek. "Oh. Leah wants to know if you want to get out," she asked.

"Yeah. Why not. For a minute though because I'll probably be tired after work," she suggested. Penny and Alexis left the restaurant, walking in separate directions back to their offices that were within walking distance from *The Eatery*.

"Where did you go tonight?" Tom asked, as he undressed, standing over Penny's bed and looking down at her. Penny had on a beige, lace and satin negligee and nothing else, as she laid on her bed waiting on her lover to join her. Tom was a good pussy eater but wasn't that great otherwise because he always came fast. He was only good for a few strokes for a few minutes and would be snoring a few seconds later.

He took off everything revealing his nice toned body that was amazing given the fact that he was in his fifties. He kissed Penny slowly as she moaned, slowly making his way to her neck and then nibbled on her ear as he continued his way down her body to his favorite area. Penny reached over and grabbed her phone and looked at her texts as she pushed him down toward her vagina. She was ready for him to suck, fuck, come and go home.

She had been down this road with him too many times to count and was just going through the motions. He was generous and wasn't very demanding of her so she continued on with the affair that she profited from. But if he even so much as suggested that he wanted to be with her full time, he would see just how uncommitted to him she was. "Oh Tom," she moaned, as she read a text from Solid, one of her other lovers. Solid had sent her a *dick pic* and she stared at it wishing that it was him between her legs instead of Tom. Tom was good but Solid was better.

"Ohhh yes baby," she moaned, as she continued flipping texts. Tom gave her fifteen minutes of fabulous head then fucked her for just a few minutes before coming, rolling over and falling asleep. Penny rolled her eyes. She wished he was a better lover. She liked head but she loved dick. Eating her pussy for fifteen minutes then fucking her for five, was not going to get it if he ever wanted Penny to consider a more serious relationship with him. But Tom knew better. He was aware that he was not her only lover. He had sat outside her single unit apartment and caught the glimpse of a man, in the shadows who appeared to kiss her on the cheek as he left one night at two o'clock in the morning.

Penny texted; *You up.* After a few minutes Alexis replied; *I wasn't. I am now. My phone woke me up. What's wrong.* Penny replied; *Just wanted to talk. Paula call you back yet?* Alexis replied; *No. She never did. I think you're right. I shouldn't try so hard when it comes to her. I'm not going to beg to be in someone's life. I miss her but if she can't even call me back after I've called her, then I just won't worry about it. Not calling anymore. Meet me over mom's tomorrow after work. I got her a gift for her birthday. Did you remember this time?* she asked. Penny replied; *Yes. Of course I did. I'll see you there.*

The next morning Penny got up and jumped in the shower. Tom had only left four hours before and she smelled of him. She often wondered how he was able to stay so long, throughout the night without worrying about going home. She wondered why his wife allowed the behavior. She believed that money or not, a woman needed to have limitations. Penny turned on her music as she took her time taking a shower. Her relaxed, *take my time* attitude, was often the reason why she could never be on time to work. As she got out the shower, she dressed in a beautiful royal blue dress, black leather YSL heels and walked out her door.

Penny walked through the lobby, causing a stir as usual, when she saw the gentleman from the day before who helped her pick up the papers she dropped. She smiled at him and stood next to him as they both, along with ten other people, waited for the elevator. They boarded the elevator and he stood next to her and stared at her side profile as she tried to look forward. She was turned on as she pictured the nastiest, *naked in the sack* images of him and her, all while trying to remain calm and appear unfazed.

"You forgot this when you were picking up those papers," he said, as he passed her a small piece of paper. She took it and looked at it. It read; *Call me,* with a number on it and the name *Camron* written under the number. She smiled and looked back at him as she left him on the elevator, headed to her office. *Damn she fine,* he thought, as he watched her sashay down to her office.

Penny went to her desk, still smiling as she put her purse away and sat down. She looked at her to do list and then turned on her computer so she could begin her day. Tom walked by and smiled like a kid in a candy store and Penny smiled back. She looked up and saw Leah approaching. "Pen. I had a ball yesterday. Girl. I met this guy and I already spoke with him at least three times. Do you remember the guy that kept asking me to dance?" Leah said, grinning and looking around. "Yeah Leah. I remember," Penny replied. "Wait. What is going on with you. Why you in a daze. Ok. What's up?" Leah said. "Nothing. It's just. There's this guy," she replied.

"Oh shit! What! You always meeting someone. Who? Give me all the deets Pen," she said, as she waited in anticipation of some great "love at first sight" story. She envied Penny's love life. Penny always met the most handsome, eligible bachelors around and Leah liked living vicariously through her.

Leah was attractive and petite and was more shy when it came to men even though she wished she wasn't. She wanted to be a temptress like Penny, she just didn't have it in her. "I don't know him. I just saw him for the first time yesterday. Fine! Fine! Fine! Leah. I mean... fine like get down on your knees in an alley fine," she said, looking at the excitement on Leah face. "He's brown skinned with the sexiest eyes. He got a mustache and beard and smells fucking insane. I don't know what cologne he is wearing but it's making me want to rape his ass," she said, laughing and looking at his number. "I'm calling him. Tonight!"

Penny left *TNT Investments* and headed for her mother's house. She called Alexis to see if she was in route there as well. "Hey. I'm on the freeway," Alexis said. "Me too. Probably right behind you," she replied. "Alexis," she exclaimed. "What Pen. I know that voice. You met someone," she stated. "Yep. Fine as hell. Already talked to him. He coming over tonight," she said. "Pen please try not to fuck him on the first date. Please. Let the man enjoy your company," she teased. "Oh shut up. You getting ready to have cob webs again. You probably not going to fuck for another six months. So, I'm going to fuck him for me and you," she said, laughing.

"What! Don't fuck him for my sake. I get nothing out of that," she joked, then continued. "And anyway. Don't mind me. I'm ok until I get married. I want something more. You know that," she continued, her tone turning more serious. "I know. You'll find what you're looking for. Everyone you go out with falls in love with yo ass. But I know you want something special," Penny said.

She joked with her sister a lot about men but she also respected the fact that Alexis, as beautiful as she was, always did things on her own with no help. She could easily live off of a man. She had several suitors try to turn her into a housewife. But Alexis was a romantic and believed in true love and wouldn't allow a man to *buy* her. She built her company, dollar by dollar, with her own money and hard work, not from a handout. "Well, I'll see you in a minute," Alexis said, as they hung up.

Alexis and Penny talked with their mother Priscilla for hours, laughing eating and drinking wine until it started getting late. Priscilla was a beauty even still as she was celebrating her fifty ninth birthday. She lived a nice quiet comfortable life thanks to her daughters including Paula who had started sending money to her mother to help with her expenses.

Penny laughed with them and grabbed the wine to pour herself one more glass before heading home. She looked down at her phone and saw that Camron had called. She picked up her phone and walked to the back bedroom so she could have some privacy and called him back.

"Hey," she said. "Hey. You almost done at your moms," he asked. "Yeah," she replied, smiling from ear to ear. "Ok. I'll be on my way when you text me. I got us something to eat too so don't worry about food," he said. Penny hung up and stared off. *Damn. He likes to feed a woman too!*

Penny walked back into the front room and sat down. She smiled at Alexis who looked at her and raised her eyebrow. She knew what the smile meant. Time to go. "Ok, ma. We're going to get out of here. Do you need anything before we go?" Alexis asked. "No baby. I'm good. Both of you drive safe. Especially you Penny. Don't think I didn't see all that wine you drank," her mother expressed. "Ma. I'm good. I promise. I'll call you to let you know I made it in," Penny stated. The two left their mothers headed to their homes, kissing each other on the cheek and getting in their cars.

Penny pulled up to a waiting Camron who was sitting on her small step with flowers in his hand. She smiled before she even got out of the car. *Fuck! Ok Penny. Calm down. He's fine but you have to be cool. No fucking,* she thought, as she opened her car door. "Hey Camron," she said, as she approached her door. "Hey," he said, grinning and looking way to fine for her to try and be modest. If "no fucking" would happen, it would be due to the fact that he stayed in his lane and didn't cross over.

Penny walked up to her door and slowly opened it. She was feeling the wine but Penny could handle shots of tequila. So the wine would not be able to intoxicate her on a level of her having no control. "Oh, these are beautiful," she said, taking the flowers and walking to her kitchen. She cut on her lights and then her tv. "Make yourself comfortable," she said, as she returned and took the bag of food he had in his other hand.

Camron sat down and watched her walk away looking at her ass and hoping to not lose his cool. Penny was shaped like a vixen and he was smitten. She opened the food and took out two plates and asked him if he wanted her to fix his plate. Camron got up and walked to her kitchen and over to her. "I couldn't hear you. What did you say?" he said, looking intensely in her eyes. "Um I said...I was asking...If you were hungry," she said, looking back at him, with a mesmerizing and sexy look in her eyes.

Camron walked right up to her and started kissing her. He pushed her to the counter and then lifted her up on it. Penny kissed him like she hadn't kissed a man in a year. He smelled good, his breath was delicious, and he looked like her knight in shining armor. "Wait Camron. We should wait. We have to get to know each other," she said. "Yeah you're right. You're right. I'm sorry. I couldn't help myself. I've been dreaming of you," he said and he stepped back and paused, looking at her and trying to control his desires.

She possibly could have pushed him off and waited but telling her he dreamed of her melted her heart and she would have to wait until later to ask all the questions she wanted to know. For now, she had to have him. Penny pulled him back to her and the two kissed fervently like they were lost lovers reunited for the first time. Penny unbuttoned her blouse, exposing her breast which Camron rubbed lightly then sucked on. He kissed and sucked her nipples then came back up and dove his tongue in her mouth. Penny moaned as he then reached under her skirt and pulled her thong to the side.

"Camron stop! We really should stop," she said, as she continued kissing him. He could tell she really didn't want him to stop and so he rubbed her clit which made her moan and pull him closer to her. He lifted her up and put her down, pushing her to the wall as they continued to kiss. Penny pushed him away and proceeded to her room with him unbuttoning his shirt and following her back. She pulled her skirt down and looked at him as she removed her shirt. Penny watched as he rubbed his dick at the site of her undressing and she was turned on even more. She crawled across her bed on her hands and knees and he grabbed her and pulled her back and put a condom on then entered her from the back and pounded her as he moaned and closed his eyes.

"Camron damn...Ohhh," she moaned, as she arched her back so he could go deeper. She loved the way he fucked her and she knew decided at that moment, that she would be fucking him from then on. He was magnetic. Sexy. Charming. And completely irresistible. "I...don't want anything serious. But I do, ahhh, want...to see you," she said, as she tried talking. Camron smiled. He stopped and looked at her. "Whatever you want. I want you. I want more that to fuck. But I'll wait," he said. Penny looked at his mouth. Then his eyes. She could see she would be abandoning her attempt at keeping some distance. He was deliciously masculine and sensitive all in one. The perfect combination. She regretted trying to put up walls.

"I haven't been in anything serious. Just don't hurt me. I can't take it," she said. "Me either. I won't. Do you know I've been thinking of you every day. No way am I here to hurt you. Now shut up woman," he said with a chuckle. Penny laughed then pulled him to her lips. She loved the way he handled her. He would have to find power. She was a lot of woman.

"Camron... damn baby," she said, as she moaned and pulled the sheets tight between her fingers. Camron was skilled and gave her pussy the best thrashing it had had in a long time. Solid was her favorite lover but not anymore. Camron flipped her over and laid on top of her and finished what he started, pulling her legs up to her head and diving deep into her pussy until she screamed his name. He came a few minutes after he knew she came and laid on her a few minutes before rolling over and falling to sleep.

Penny woke up the next morning to the smell of coffee and got up and grabbed her silk robe. "Hey," she said, as she walked into the kitchen. It was Saturday and she didn't have to be to work. Camron walked up to her and kissed her. "I made you a cup," he said, going back towards her sink. Penny smiled. He was comfortable in her apartment. She watched as he used her Keurig and made her a cup of White Chocolate Cappuccino. He handed it to her and she kissed him and walked over and sat down.

"Want to do something today?" he asked. Penny shook her head yes and continued sipping her cappuccino. She liked the way he made her feel. This was a first. She was actually letting a man stay the next day after having stayed all night. Penny usually came up with some excuse to get rid of her date by morning. But not Camron. She hated to admit it but she had hoped he wasn't ready to go. She wanted him to stay.

Chapter Four – Paula

P

aula sat at her desk, sipping tea and looking over her schedule. She opened emails and took a few calls as she sat there looking out the window. Paula glanced down at her wedding ring. She twirled the Tiffany, platinum and diamond ring her handsome, sexy and sophisticated husband had given to her. Hers was a charmed life that any woman would want to live. And Paula's life was the real deal. A husband who delivered on every want, every need. A rich, self-made businessman who was a loyal husband and a dedicated father. Paula sat there thinking how lucky she was. She also thought about her heart and how empty it still felt. Paula felt empty because she was not living in her truth. Something her lover told her she should do and now she was contemplating.

"Mrs. Wade. Your three o'clock is here," the secretary said into the phone. Paula sighed as she gathered her things for her quick but important meeting.

"Thanks Miriam. I'll be there shortly," she said, checking her phone before walking to the door and down the hall. She had a meeting with a small start-up company looking to revamp their web site and consult with her on how to polish their look and draw more clients.

Paula was an advertising consultant and web site designer and had secured this client on her own without the help of her husband Rome. She originally leaned on her husband's expertise. She'd met him working as an intern at his company when the two fell in love and were married a short time later. A lot of the women at his firm were jealous and envied Paula for being able to pull off what some of them had tried to do with the super sexy, fine as hell, thirty five year old bachelor. He'd dated only one other woman at his office. Rome tried to avoid dating at his place of business and had sworn against it.

Paula was hired by his cousin who immediately thought of him when she hired Paula. She liked her style and she saw something in Paula that she thought would make her generous and handsome cousin a good mate. Paula was highly educated and self-sufficient. She was a light brown skinned beauty with long straight hair cut into a shoulder length bob, a nice figure and was dressed impeccably.

She wore light, natural make up and had the longest natural eyelashes. She was a beautiful and classy, twenty nine year old woman at the time. She carried herself like an up and coming business woman and so his cousin hired her without much of an interview. And her plan worked. Rome was immediately smitten with the beautiful yet elusive Paula and they were married a year later.

But Rome never told about the fairytale that ended before it even began. How Paula was pregnant in just a few short months and how she basically abandoned the marriage after giving birth to their son. How she had basically started her business with his help and pretty much was living with him in more of a roommate type of relationship than one of husband and wife. Rome struggled with the reasons behind his wife's lack of interest in him romantically or sexually and tried to persevere. He had a young son to raise and that was his main focus.

Paula came home most nights except on her business travels which were often and so he dealt with the distance within their union. He had hoped to rekindle what he'd lost with her and tried in vain to get close to her but always seemed to fall short. A friend he confided in told him initially that it was postpartum depression and she would get better with time. He believed it and waited her out. She seemed to get better but their relationship didn't seem to improve. And so, they lived their mundane lives, working and going home to a fake, unloving and lackluster family life. Their only reason to continue in the charade was their son Romy.

"Hi. I'm Paula Wade," she said, as she shook the hand of the scraggly bearded, petite white man and his even scragglier business partner. Paula was snobbish and would usually look down on people dressed as these men were. But Paula was well aware that these two were millionaires with a new start-up company and she planned on gaining their trust and getting their business. Paula was elegant, sophisticated and always tried not to come across as the snob that she was. She sat in her meeting that went longer than she had anticipated.

After a few hours of going through some possible web designs, she shook the hands of her newly acquired clients and walked them to the front door. "Thanks again. I'll get right on the initial designs of the front page and then start adding all the information and click features. I should have something for you to see and approve in a week. So, give my secretary some dates that your schedule is open so we can meet again," she said.

Paula shook the men's hand and watched as they exited then walked back to her office and put hand sanitizer on. She sat at her desk and proceeded to add information into the web page she was working on for another client when her phone buzzed. She looked at the caller i.d. and saw that Rome was calling. *I'm going to have to call him back*, she thought, as she sat her phone back down.

P

aula walked into an empty house and kicked her shoes off. She knew that Rome had taken Romy to a kid's play with his buddies and their kids and she was glad to have the house to herself. She walked through her large estate slowly, inspecting room by room, making sure their housekeeper had done a good job. Paula was particular and if there had been even a hint of dust, she would not have been too happy. But their housekeeper had been with them for the five years that they stayed at the large six-bedroom estate and so she knew Paula well. She had perfected her job over the years in an effort to avoid Paula's disappointment and request to redo the entire room, front to back.

"Mmmm," Paula moaned, as she rubbed her feet. She kicked her other shoe off and laid back on her stacked pillows. Her long day would end in a bubble bath and a cup of hot tea. Her house was quiet for once. It was obvious her husband had taken their son somewhere and she would have a moment to herself. Paula grabbed her phone and called her lover, who lived in London.

"Hi babe. What you doing?" Paula said to her female friend and lover of four years. Amy was a former coworker who had moved back to London after living in the US for a few years. She and Paula had started an affair right under Rome's nose at his company *Fusion Digital.*

"Hi baby. I miss you. Why are you just now calling me?" Amy replied. Paula apologized and immediately made excuses for her long absences and unanswered calls. She told Amy how much she missed her and the two spoke of plans to see one another. But there was a problem. They were still hiding. Paula was still unwilling to tell her husband the truth. Amy was growing tired and desperate as she had waited on Paula to finally tell Rome about them so that they could be together.

"When are you going to tell him Paula. I don't want to wait for you forever. If it's not ever going to happen then just tell me now so I can move on with my life," Amy complained. Paula wiped her eyes. It was the first time she'd cried in a long time. Paula was tough and she didn't cry easily. But she was hopelessly in love with Amy and was upset at the thought of losing her companion. Amy had been a tough tomboy all her life and had realized early, that she liked women. She had never been with a man. It was always so clear to her.

But Paula did date men and suppressed her desires until much later. She first noticed her attraction to women when she was fourteen but she was such a perfectionist and so concerned with people's opinion of her that she suppressed her desires and continued to date men even though her heart wasn't in it.

As Paula and Amy continued talking, she heard the door open. She heard Romy running through the house calling *mommy, mommy*. "Amy. Honey. I have to go," she rushed off the phone, blowing kisses into the phone as she hung up. "Hi Romy," she said, reaching down to pick up her son and swoop him up. Romy was just three years old and was a smart, active kid who kept Paula and Rome busy. He was the most important thing in his father's life and the sole reason Rome had not asked for a divorce from his uninvolved, distant wife.

Rome walked in and kissed Paula on the cheek as she looked away and kissed her son. She was cordial but nothing more. They hadn't made love in over six months and she knew he wouldn't wait much longer. She dreaded the thought and couldn't imagine herself intimate with him. She was far from that. She was totally consumed with thoughts of Amy. She was borderline obsessed with her and she was thinking every day, of a way to tell him the obvious. That she was no longer in the relationship with him and wanted out.

"I'm going on a business trip to London," she said, as Rome unbuttoned his Zegna shirt and took his LeCoultre watch off and placed it in his glass and wood jewelry case. "Ok. When are you leaving?" he asked. "Saturday morning," Paula replied, leaving the room and taking her son to his room to prepare him for bed time. She sat the toddler down and he ran around, full of energy, not appearing to be ready for bed. She could hear Rome walk into the bathroom and close the door.

Paula looked at her son and got emotional. She loved him but she knew she would have to leave him behind if she wanted to start a new life with Amy. Rome would never allow her to take his son to London. Paula however, was prepared to leave Romy with his dad where he could get the best care and love a kid could have. Paula, although well intentioned, was not the best mom and she knew it.

It was Rome, not her, who got up in the middle of the night when he was an infant for those early morning feeds. It was Rome who was there for every bump and bruise, while Paula was off with her lover or somewhere running from her responsibilities. She was only somewhat affectionate with Romy, showering him momentarily with kisses then turning her attention on her own wants and desires and pulling away. Paula had a habit of turning her back on the ones who loved and needed her. She had shunned her mother and her sisters and moved to New York, calling them yearly to check in and eventually, not checking in at all. She was selfish in that regard.

Rome emerged from the shower and walked to his kitchen. He had on a tee shirt and pajama pants and smelled wonderful. Rome was brown skinned with a mustache and goatee that laid on his face like velvet. He was sexy times ten and was built like that of a man who worked out and took the time to create a physique worth melting over. But Paula looked at him as though he were see-thru glass. Rome knew women all over the globe melted at the sight of him, just not his wife.

"You hungry," he asked Paula. He had bought home some carry out from their favorite restaurant and was fixing himself a plate.

"No, I ate," she yelled from their room, as she prepared to take a shower. Romy was asleep and she was ready to shower and go to bed. Paula got in bed and pulled the covers over her body. She knew Rome still desired her and she worked overtime to keep him at bay. Rome came to their room and saw that Paula had fell asleep. Paula laid there with her eyes closed and was actually pretending to be asleep. He sat on the bed and sighed. This would be yet another night of no love making. Rome got under the sheets and shut his lamp off and went to sleep.

Paula got up the next day and ran her morning the way she normally did. She walked through her home, inspecting everything for cleanliness and then proceeded to take a shower. She then said bye to her husband and left him with the responsibility of getting their son to day care or to his family's home so he could go to work. Paula made her drive to work stopping at Starbucks on the way. She made a call to her office as she waited in line. "Hey Miriam. Can you tell me who I'm meeting with this morning? I know I had you switch things around but I can't remember which changes I made," she stated, as she pulled up the drive through to order a Carmel Macchiato. "You're meeting with Damon Farley from Prizms Digital," she replied. "Ok that's all I wanted," she said.

Paula was waiting in line behind two other cars when her phone rang. She looked at the caller i.d. and saw it was Rome. Paula looked out the window and sighed. *What does he want now!*

"Hello," she answered.

"Hey what you doing?" he asked.

"Nothing Rome. What's wrong?" she asked.

"Nothing. Can't I call to talk to my wife? You left so fast this morning. I didn't even get a chance to see your face." Paula sighed again.

"I said bye. Didn't you hear me," she said.

"No," he replied holding the phone.

"Sorry. What is it?" she asked.

"Paula. We need to talk. This talk is long overdue. You know things are not right between us. They haven't been for a while. I can tell you want a divorce but you're afraid to tell me. Is that what's going on? Tell me?" he said, sounding frustrated at the state of their relationship.

Paula held the phone and then pulled her car out of the line and off to the side. "Rome. Let's not have this conversation here on the phone. Not now. Can we talk when we get home tonight," she replied, sounding frustrated.

"No. I want to talk now," he demanded.

"I can't. I have all kinds of feelings that I can't put into words right now. I'll see you tonight so we can talk," she said before hanging up on him. Paula looked at the Starbucks line that was now, almost a half block long, and decided to pull off. She shook her head but then called her lover Amy to get her mind right.

"Hello," she answered.

"Oh Amy! I can't! I can't do this anymore. I'm telling him tonight. You're right. He needs to know. I have to tell him. He called me asking if I wanted a divorce," she said, as a tear rolled down her perfectly made up face. Amy looked off. It was the moment she'd hoped for. Her lover to be honest and come clean. They were in love. Had been for years. It was time.

"And you told him yeah right," Amy responded.

"No. Not yet. I didn't say anything. I told him we'll talk tonight. I promise you tonight is the night. I'm telling him what's going on. He has to be told."

R

ome walked into *Fusion Digital*, one of two companies he owned, quiet and distracted. He walked past his secretary and spoke but didn't say much else. She immediately noticed his demeanor because that wasn't like the Rome she knew. The man she knew always had something to say. He was always friendly and approachable. Rome was a great employer in fact. He was stern and steadfast with his business dealings and fair with his employees. He was well liked boss and was overly generous, especially with his female employees. He allowed his pregnant employees to take extended maternity leaves and be out for up to six months without worry of losing their jobs.

Their office was flooded with applications seeking employment all the time because of his generosities and also their popular company affairs. They threw quarterly parties at a lavish ball to celebrate the birthdays that fell within the three months and no expense was spared. His secretary Erin, hated when he wasn't in a good mood. She cared about him, even had a crush on him, but her feelings for him were more based on the fact that he hired her when no one else would.

She had no college education, no real experience and no car when she first started at the company. She worked her way up to his personal secretary, took classes in basic computer functions and was able to contribute more to his company. He rewarded her with bonus checks which she used to get a car. And even though he was once the most eligible bachelor around, he was committed to Paula and appeared faithful and happy and she respected that. Erin admired him for that but she still desired him.

Erin went to Rome's office to go over his schedule and see what he needed for the day. She knocked on the door even though the door was open and he waved her in. She walked in as he talked on the phone. After a few minutes, Rome got off the phone and Erin sat down, apprehensive about the meeting because of his obvious troubled mood. "So, I have the list of perspective clients and which sales people were assigned to the lead," she said, handing him the list.

"Um Mr. Wade. Is everything ok? You seem distracted," she said.

"I am. But it's ok. Just got a lot to do that's all," he replied. Erin's secret crush had grown into a full-blown fantasy over the years that she indulged whenever she was around him. She loved to look in his gorgeous face and imagine him doing all kinds of things to her. He always smelled good and he always looked good. She rarely saw him repeat his clothes and imagined that he had a Macy's sized closet at his home filled with the best suits, shirts and shoes. And Erin didn't miss the fact that she could see his dick print through most of his pants and that fueled her desires even more.

"And this is the list of clients that need a follow up call and who the assigned sales person is." She said, handing him the pile of leads.

Rome took each list from her and looked over the names. He was oblivious to her crush and thought of her as like a little sister. Rome planned on meeting with each salesperson individually to see what their plan was to land the clients and make the sale. As Erin stood up to leave Rome asked her to look into flight information to London and check all the swankiest, most expensive hotels there. He told her to call each one and ask if there were reservations for a Paula Wade for the weekend and to keep quiet about it. Erin told him she would but then made a face when she left his office. He was checking up on his wife and Erin tried to put the pieces of the puzzle together. *So that's why he's so quiet. That bitch having an affair!*

Erin came back into Rome office several hours later with the name of the hotel that Paula was staying at. She handed him the paper and walked out. He said thank you to her as she neared his door. He was aware that he'd never asked her to do something that personal for him. Rome looked at the paper that read; *The Franklin* and crumbled it in his hand. He had a feeling that the last-minute trip involved Paula hooking up for an affair with some guy and he was determined to get to the bottom of it.

S

aturday appeared the same as any other Saturday except Paula was packing to leave for her trip. She'd had a long night and they never did have their talk after the day he called when she was at Starbucks. And Paula felt bad for the millionth time. Rome tried to make love to her the night before and she lied to him and told him she was not feeling well. She got out of their bed and went into another room to avoid his touch.

Rome stayed up all night frustrated and rubbing his dick trying to get the urge to go away. He was unsuccessful at his jack off attempt. He was too mad and too jealous to complete it. He ended up trying to fall to sleep with a hard on that seemed like it took forever to go down. But she continued packing, feeling guilty and trying to come up with the words to say to end her marriage on a good note.

But Paula was a coward. She ran from things instead of facing them. She ran from her family back at home out of anger towards her father, mother and Penny. She ran from her first boyfriend when he told her he loved her. She ran from her jobs when the pressure got to great. Her whole life was one big marathon and she was tired.

"Rome. My limo will be here soon," she said. Paula continued preparing for her trip, totally unaware that Rome himself was leaving for the airport in two hours. He was bound for the same destination and so he let her morning go as she had planned.

He was curious as to why she didn't ask him to take her to the airport but figured her lover may be there. He didn't want to confront her at the airport and miss the opportunity to see who her lover was and also give her the chance to lie and make up a story. He wanted to surprise her and show up at her door and catch her in the act.

Paula grabbed her bags and left the house when she heard the horn blow. She kissed Romy and rolled her suitcase down the hall as she made her way toward her front door. Paula looked around but didn't see Rome. He usually carried her bags to the car for her but was nowhere in sight. She picked up her bags and left out, headed for the airport.

Paula was enjoying London as she travelled around looking at what the city had to offer its visitors. She was already having a ball with her lover as they walked through parks and visited a few museums. They spent most of the day going site seeing as Amy showed Paula around. They stopped by her family's estate, eating at the best restaurants the city had to offer before going back to *The Franklin*. Paula made a few calls back home and even conducted business over the phone.

Amy was a wealthy financial advisor who had started her own company after leaving the US a few years prior. Her company took off with the help of her father and some sound investments and she was making just as much money as Rome was. They were in their room for several hours before Paula heard a light knock on the door. She looked over at Amy who was sleep. She wondered for a moment but then assumed that Amy had ordered room service again. She had mentioned wanting something sweet and so Paula assumed it was a tray of deserts. "Coming," she said as she walked to the suite's door.

Paula opened the door and her mouth dropped open at the shock of her husband standing there. He looked totally distraught and inconsolable. His eyes were red as if he had cried at some point. But the red was from upset and fury not tears. Rome never cried over Paula and he wasn't about to start.

"Rome. What are you doing here?" she said, angry but trying to hide her feelings. She wasn't sure if she could trust the moment. This was out of character for him. He stood there motionless and since he was no longer easy to read, she feared him going off and so she didn't push his buttons.

"No Paula. What are you doing here?" he said, as he walked past her.

Rome looked around and then stopped at the door to the bedroom and then turned around to face Paula.

"What the fuck is going on," he shouted. Paula put her finger up to her lips in a gesture for him to stop shouting but he could care less at that moment.

"Don't you fucking shush me. Who the fuck is that? Are you fucking a woman?" he asked.

His voice was loud and Amy woke up and jumped out of bed. She walked into the sitting area slowly, looking back and forth between Paula and Rome. Paula teared up and then looked at Amy and asked her to leave. Amy went into the room and grabbed her shoes and walked towards the door. "You need to tell him Paula," she said, as she closed the door behind her.

"That's Amy who used to work for me. Yeah, she's right. You need to tell me," he said, sitting down on the couch.

Paula paced the floor, unable to speak at first. She wasn't afraid of what he would do. She was afraid of the damage she was about to cause. He didn't deserve what she was about to say but she knew she had to say it.

"Ok. I'm just going to come out and say it. Yes, I want a divorce. I'm in love with her and I need to be here with her," she said. Rome sat speechless and looking around as if in a daze. He wasn't sure he heard her right. He could see her lips moving but he had to be dreaming because he did not just hear his wife say she was in love with a woman and that she was leaving. Rome stood up and looked her directly in her eyes.

"You will not take my son," he said, looking angry and hurt by her actions.

"I know. I wasn't going to. He needs you. He's better off with you," she said, as she wiped the tears from her eyes.

Rome walked to the window and looked out at the picturesque scene. The romantic view that was not his to enjoy.

"Did you ever love me?" he asked. Paula walked to the couch and sat down.

"I don't know. Maybe," she replied.

"Maybe?" he said, with a chuckle as he couldn't believe his ears. He looked over at her and then walked towards her.

"Then a divorce is what you'll have. Don't come back to the house. And call if you want to see Romy, I'll make some sort of arrangement," he said. Rome walked to the door and slammed it closed. He took the stairs and walked through the lobby, eye balling Amy he walked past.

Rome boarded the plane and stared out the window most of the flight turning every drink and food choice down. He held onto a bottle of water and drank from it as he tried to wrap his head around what had just happened. The flight attendants were whispering about the gorgeous man in first class who seemed despondent and wouldn't eat. They had approached him several times trying to see if he had changed his mind but he continued to send them away.

By the time his final flight landed, Rome was mentally drained and exhausted. He got in his car and drove, as his heavy eyes struggled to stay open. He barely made it to his home in the Carnegie Hill section of Manhattan. He walked in and was greeted by Romy who was still up despite it being eleven o'clock at night. "I'm sorry Mr. Wade. He wouldn't go to sleep. He kept getting out of bed," the housekeeper Ann stated. "That's alright. Thanks Ann. I'll take it from here," he said, as he hugged his son and then promised to read him a story before bed.

It wasn't long before little Romy was asleep in his father's arms. Rome had read his son a bedtime story and was ready to turn in for the night. He turned out his light and turned on the nightlight as he left, glancing back at his son as he closed the door slowly. Rome went in his room and plopped down on the bed. His mind was deep in thought as he tried to make sense of what he had just discovered.

He wondered how he missed the signs. What happened between them that resulted in his wife abandoning what they had. He would have to explain to a three year old that his mom would be moving out. Rome shook his head. He knew Romy would be ok eventually. The baby gravitated towards him more, which was no fault of his own. Paula was always unavailable, and so the toddler would eventually look for Rome. But the baby was still attached to his mother because of his age, and so Rome struggled with how he would deal with her absence. *I'll call my father and get his advice*, he thought, as he prepared to shower.

Chapter Five – The Request

P

aula and Amy decided to leave the hotel and go to Amy's condo. Paula had spent days in a quiet somber mood that Amy tried to help her through. The women talked about their plans. Then talked about little Romy and they talked about Rome.

Paula told Amy everything. She told her details about her past and how she felt about her family and the fact that she was ashamed of them her whole life. She told Amy that she didn't communicate with them and that her past was horrible and shameful and she wanted no memories of it. Amy listened as Paula spoke about her sisters and how she only really got along with her youngest sister Pebbles. She shared stories about how she felt with regards to her middle sister who brought shame to the family by being promiscuous and she told her how she caught her sister sitting on their step fathers lap and that there was something weird about that moment.

She told Amy she always believed that Penny was flirtatious with their dad and caused him to drink excessively until he killed himself in a car crash. She said her mother knew things and that her mother went crazy after the father passed away, which she blamed on Penny as well. She stated that Pebbles was so close to Penny that when she decided to cut Penny off, she cut Pebbles off too, only talking to her occasionally until she finally ceased all communication.

Paula revealed her deepest secrets that surprised Amy and the two tried to get a handle on what was going on and how Paula should proceed. Paula stated she had a plan but didn't know if it would work. She stated that it was risky and not what a normal thinking person would do but that she would proceed and let things happen however they played out.

Alexis was at home nursing a sore ankle from a roller skating mishap that she had while roller blading with Penny. Her phone buzzed as she lay there with an ice pack on her ankle. She was mad at herself for sitting down and leaving her phone four feet away on the kitchen counter. *Damn!* she said, as she tried to get up. She hopped over to the counter and was shocked to see Paula calling. She hadn't heard from Paula since the attempted call a few months earlier and was puzzled. She answered it, happy to finally be hearing back from her.

"Hello," she exclaimed, waiting to hear the voice of her darling older sister.

"Hi Pebbles," Paula said, sounding happy and excited to be talking to her.

"Paula. Oh my goodness. It's been so long. What happened to you calling me back? You called me a few months ago but then you never answered when I tried to call you back," she asked.

"I'm sorry Pebs. I got busy. So much is going on. So much I have to tell you. How's mom?" she asked.

"She's good. And so is Penny," she stated. Paula paused then continued talking.

"Pebs you got a minute to talk about something serious. If not, I'll call you back but I have to talk to you," she said.

"Of course I do. I have a company now Paula. It's called Alexis Allen Designs. I'm not working from home anymore. It's not open on the weekends. And I have a lot to tell you too. I changed my name to Alexis. I don't want to be called Pebbles anymore. But I can talk now. What's wrong?" she asked.

"You changed your name legally?" Paula asked.

"Yes. I meant to tell you so you can get used to calling me that," Alexis replied.

"Why Pebs! What's wrong with your name. I mean, Alexis is your middle name so it's still your name. But why the switch?" she asked.

"I guess I felt some type of way when dad died and since he was the one who gave me my middle name, I decided to honor his memory and make it my first name," she replied. Paula was silent. She was speechless as to her sisters reason. She thought they all disliked their mean, overbearing and drunken father. But she realized that her youngest sister had a different take on it, probably because she was the only one who was his biological daughter.

"Ok. Alexis it is," Paula said, as she sighed. It was time to stop the small talk and get to the favor she needed. One she hoped her sister would agree to do.

"I have a favor to ask. But now I feel guilty asking you because I didn't know you had started your own design company. I thought you were still working from home," Paula stated, as she held the phone, struggling to ask her sister the favor. She wasn't sure that Alexis could do it and she wasn't sure of the repercussions after the fact.

"What is it Paula? You have never asked anything of me. I miss you. You're still my sister. I don't care that you don't call. I only care that you're calling now. Whatever you need, I'm there for you." she said.

Paula paused and sighed. Alexis could hear her breathing, and guessed she was nervous. She was perplexed and patiently waiting for the news that was making her usually put together sister, edgy and tense. Paula was never at a loss of words with her.

"I need you to go to my home in New York and stay there and help Rome take care of the baby while I'm gone. I'm in London and I can't go home right now," she said. Alexis was in total shock. *Did she just ask me to move into her house! What the fuck! I didn't hear her right*, she thought.

"What? You need me to do what?" she asked, perplexed and stressing about what she thought she heard. Alexis wanted to hear it again. It was not a request, it was a life changing event.

"Did you say, move to your house?" she continued.

"Yes," she replied.

Alexis held the phone. She held the phone as she tried to think clearly about her sisters' request and consider if it was even possible. She didn't mind going to visit and check up on things, but move in. This was a difficult order to fill.

"Paula. I don't know. That's asking a lot. I mean. I can go there for a few days maybe but actually move in…How long are we talking?' she asked.

"Sixty days maybe. Please Alexis! I'll compensate you. We have money. Money's no object. How much you want?" she asked.

"It's not that Paula. My company is new. I'm still growing. Being gone sixty days could be disastrous to my bottom line. I have employees. They will get nervous and quit if I'm not around. It will look as though I abandoned my company," she replied.

"They will stand behind you as long as they see their getting paid and as long as they hear from you often. You can fly back after a few weeks to show your face and let them see that you still have control of your business. Please Alexis. I have no one else. I need you," she begged.

Alexis held the phone again. Paula was sounding desperate and Alexis found it hard to say no to her sister whom she barely talked to and who had never asked anything of her before. Alexis thought hard, biting her nails and weighing the risks.

"Ok. Paula. But after a few weeks, at some point, I'll need to leave and come home to check up on my office," she stated.

"I love you Pebs. Thanks. I'll call you tomorrow and you can tell me where to send your plane ticket to," she replied.

Paula called Rome the next day. She decided to tell him that her sister was going to be there and help out until she returned to the states. She wasn't prepared to go into detail. Paula figured the less he knew the better. She planned to only tell him that Alexis would be there to watch Romy and nothing more. Paula's plan consisted of more than her son but she wasn't ready to reveal anything yet.

"Hello," he answered, as he rolled over and took her call. It was four o'clock in the morning and nine o'clock in London. Rome saw that it was Paula and was surprised. He hadn't talked to her in a few days. And besides, why was he getting a call so early in the morning.

"Hey it's me," she replied.

"Yeah. What's up," he said, as he wiped his eyes and tried to get himself together.

"Rome. I have something to tell you. I know you're having some issues getting help with Romy and Ann is more of a housekeeper not a nanny. So, I called my sister Alexis and she said she would come stay there until I get back," she said. Rome sat up.

"What. I don't need help. I'll be fine. I've never even met your sister. No Paula," he said, as he closed his eyes. He was ready to go right back to sleep. Whatever his soon to be ex-wife was talking about it would have to wait.

"Ok. Look... She's already coming alright. I sent her the ticket today. Just be at the airport Monday at eleven a.m. to get her," she demanded.

"Why didn't you ask me first. You just send for her. No Paula. I'll call you when I wake up," he replied, hanging up in frustration. Rome laid back down and went right back to sleep. Paula was being Paula. Surprises at the worst times. He didn't need help. And he didn't need Paula meddling. Him and his boy were good.

R

ome woke up the next day preparing to stop by both of his offices. He needed to go to Fusion Marketing first and meet with a large prospective client and then go to Impact Digital and meet with his managers. Rome took his morning shower and dressed. Romy would be with his mother for a few days while he got his mind together and handled his business. His mother Gladys had stepped in and was watching Romy so that Rome could take care of his business without worry.

He had mentioned hiring a nanny which his mother rejected and told him to bring her grandson to her. Rome was glad she offered to watch him. He really dreaded the idea of a nanny but was prepared to do what he needed. He dressed and groomed himself as he wondered about the sister who was coming to stay at his home. Rome wasn't sure if it was a good idea.

He had mixed feelings about it although he welcomed help from family. He wondered why he didn't know her. He knew there was three of them and he always imagined that there was something fucked up about them and that's why Paula cut ties with them. Paula didn't help matters. She was vague with any information regarding them and wouldn't even provide him with their real names because she knew he would look them up on social media. He would for sure find Penny but not Pebbles.

She didn't do much by the way of social media. She had a Facebook page but it didn't have a real picture of her. It had an avatar for the longest that was eventually replaced by a picture of the front of her office building. Paula gave him nick names instead so he wouldn't be able to reach out to them. She gave him stories and painted both her sisters as women to stay away from and so he did. But now one of the *toxic sisters* was coming to stay with him and he wondered why she was inviting them into their life now. Now that she was gone.

Penny rushed with coffee in hand, down the street and toward her office building. She had to park in the parking structure two blocks down because the one she normally parked at was full. There was a new tenant leasing space in her building and they had dozens of employees and now, getting a spot in that structure would be difficult.

Dammit! she said, as some of the coffee spilled on her shoes. She could hear her phone ringing but it was way down in her purse. *Fuck!* she said, as she got closer to the building. Penny stopped and fumbled through her purse trying to locate her phone. She found it, but not in time to catch Camron calling her. She hit his number to call him back.

"Hey. You at work yet," Camron asked.

"Almost. I'm walking up now," she replied.

"Call me when you get settled. I got to ask you something," he replied.

Camron and Penny were going strong. He was the first relationship she felt completely involved in. He was over all the time and they went everywhere together. Penny had pushed Solid away and hadn't seen or spoken with him in some time, but Tom was a different story. She had yet to break anything off with him, and he was growing suspicious of her suddenly busy schedule.

Penny walked through the glass doors and toward the elevator. Camron was a lawyer and no longer worked in that building. His firm acquired their only building and had moved a month ago. She missed bumping into him. He would call her and then wait for her on the stairwell where they kissed and fondled each other before work.

When she walked in, she immediately noticed the bouquet of flowers on her desk. She smiled as she approached. She read the card that said; *To my love and the woman I will be with forever, Camron.* Penny smiled and looked up. She saw Leah approaching.

"Pen. Tom was at your desk. He read the note. He been acting funny ever since. Just being mean and demanding," Leah said, looking concerned.

"Damn! Ok... Well... He needs to calm down. He's married. He can't control who I see," Penny replied. She paused for a minute then asked if anyone else saw him read her flowers. Leah stated she didn't think so and walked back to her desk. Penny sighed. She wished Camron hadn't sent the flowers, but she also had no plans on hiding him. He had been to her office at least once to take her to lunch. She was ready to end her relationship with Tom but hadn't, out of fear of losing her job.

Penny sat down and turned her computer on. She heard her phone buzz. It was a text from Alexis that read; *Call me when you free. Something's come up.* Penny stared at her phone. She hit the button to dial Alexis. She needed to know what had come up.

"Hello," Alexis answered.

"Hey. What's wrong?" Penny asked.

"You not going to believe it. But you also going to get mad. I know you. Don't get mad," she stated.

"I won't. What is it?" she asked.

"Paula called. Remember when she called me a few months ago and I tried calling her back. Well she called again. She's been traveling to London. Well anyways... She wants me to stay at her house for a while to help with Romy while she's away," she said.

"What! No Alexis. Don't you pick up and leave. The nerve of her. She's got money. Why can't she hire a nanny or something," she replied.

"She doesn't want some strange woman. It's just for a month or so, maybe two," Alexis said.

"Two gotdamn months! No Alexis. No! Give me her number. I'll call her myself. She got a lot of fucking nerve. You are way too nice. She knew not to ask me no stupid ass bullshit like that. What about your office? What about your life? I see ain't shit changed with her. What's her number?" Penny urged.

"No Pen. Don't be like that. She needs help. I'll be ok. I'm going to go but I'll be back and forth. I won't let anything happen to my company," she replied.

Penny held the phone. She was angry. She didn't want to admit it at that moment but she'd miss her sister terribly. Alexis was her girl. Her backbone. The person who supported her no matter what. The only person who didn't judge her. What would she do without her around.

"This is not a good idea Alexis. And you don't know her family. What if her baby is a little hellion? What if her husband is some psycho? Just go for a week," she advised.

"Pen. I'll be back. I promise. You're worried that you will going to miss me or something," she stated.

"Yes! I will miss you and I don't want you to go. Fuck her," Penny replied. She tried to keep from getting too emotional. But Pebbles was her backbone. Her confidant. Not having her around, to run to, was unthinkable.

The two talked for an hour. Penny ignored everyone who came up to her desk and eventually took her call outside of the office, pacing up and down the hallway, as she spoke with Alexis. In the end, Alexis convinced her that it was a temporary thing and that she felt compelled to do it. She was leaving in a few short days and would call her when she arrived.

Chapter Six – Pitch Black

Monday morning was a hectic one for Alexis. She had packed the night before, with Penny's help and had gone over everything she wanted taken care of in her absence. She gave her secretary Sara, a list of things to do for the week and told her she would be back in a few weeks.

Alexis was nervous as she tried to think of anything she may have forgotten as far as travel items and for her business. She left Delano in charge and told him her sister had an emergency. He was reluctant to take on the responsibility. Delano didn't want to admit that he relied heavily on Alexis' expertise and positive attitude. That it was she who pulled in most every client and he feared the business faltering without her. Alexis walked around her room opening drawers to check if there was anything else she wanted at that moment. She was only taking three bags, so she would be leaving behind a lot of her personal belongings. Penny had a key and would be checking up on her place.

As Alexis walked around her condo, she heard a knock at the door. She opened it and stood there. It was Delano. Looking like a lost puppy and not saying anything.

"Why are you here Delano?" she asked. He stood for a minute.

"Why are you moving? I can't handle all this without you," he replied.

"I'm not moving. And I have to leave in a minute Delano. You can come in if you want, but I don't have time to sit and talk. My plane leaves shortly. Penny will be here soon," she said.

"You'll get there and not come back. Why do I have this feeling you won't be coming back," he replied, looking intensely at her.

"You think I would leave my business, that it took me years to build. I am coming back," she replied and paused, then continued. "Besides. I'm not leaving my mother and my sister behind."

Alexis went into her room and Delano followed. He sat on her bed and just watched her. She looked at him as she placed her toiletries bag in her carry-on bag.

"What's on your mind Delano. I can tell you have something to say. What is it?" she asked.

"I want to make love to you before you go," he said. His seductive gaze was hard to ignore. Alexis looked at him. She already knew that's what he wanted when he was at her door. She knew how he felt about her, and would have been surprised if he hadn't showed up trying to see her before she left.

Delano stood up and approached her and started kissing her. And as always, his kisses were just the thing that would break her down. Alexis became instantly horny and wanted him but she pushed him away. Penny was on her way, and she had no time.

"No Delano. We're not together anymore. No. I have to go. Penny left her apartment and she'll be here shortly. Just go," she said, looking at her phone hoping he would just turn and leave. Alexis looked up when she heard a knock on her door,

"That's her," she said, walking past him. Delano followed her, walking like a wounded pet. His head down. His ego crushed. He felt it involved a guy. And he worried even more.

"Hey Delano," Penny said, as she walked in. She smiled at him. She always thought he was handsome and thought her sister was crazy for not rekindling her relationship with him.

"Hey Pen. What's up," he said, in a melancholy voice, as he stood there staring at Alexis. She looked at him and shook her head. She knew him like a book. He was back attached to her, and he would be hard to handle if she left things the way they were. She needed him functioning at his best not missing her out the gate.

"Call me when you get there," he said, as he left out. Alexis shook her head at Penny.

"What the hell," Penny said.

"He just showed up. Again!" Alexis replied.

"You ready? You have to go," Penny urged.

The two grabbed her bags and carried them down to the car. When they got outside, Alexis saw Delano just sitting in his car. She looked at Penny.

"What! Alexis No! You will miss your plane," Penny said.

"I have time. If I don't, he'll be a wreck. I need him focused," she replied.

Alexis stared at Delano, then turned and walked back into her condo leaving the door open. Delano got out of his car and walked in. Penny sighed, then got in the car and sat there, scrolling through her phone, as she waited for the two of them to finish fucking, so Alexis could go.

"Ok. Be safe. Call me when you get there. I love you sis," Penny said, wiping her eyes as if Alexis was going to Africa for ten years.

"Stop Pen. You going to make me cry. You act like I'm never coming back," she said.

The two placed Alexis' bags on the dolly and then kissed each other on the cheek and Alexis walked to her gate. She boarded the plane and sat next to a gentleman whose smell instantly reminded her of Delano. She sat down and smiled as she reminisced on her quickie that was more passionate than any of the other sex they'd had. Delano fucked her like he would never see her again and she loved it. He had never been that passionate. *Maybe I should leave more often. He should have been fucking me that way the whole time. We would probably be further along than we are if he had,* she thought.

"You're very beautiful. What's your name?" the guy sitting next to her asked.

"Hi. I'm Alexis," she replied.

"A beautiful name for a beautiful woman," the man said, in an English accent.

She guessed that he was from Britain or somewhere in the UK.

"Where are you from?" she asked.

"England," the man said smiling at her. "You should come there. It's wonderful. I could show you around," he said.

"I couldn't but thanks anyway." Alexis looked at her magazine and continued to engage in small talk as she relaxed during her flight. She continued to think about Delano and was surprised that she actually realized she would miss him. Seeing him everyday at her office and having the upper hand in their *on again/off again* relationship, had resulted in her taking him for granted.

Rome prepared to be at the airport early in case her flight arrived sooner than expected. Paula had given him the details of her airline and arrival time and he was ready to walk out the door. He was nervous. He still wasn't convinced that it was a good idea to have some strange woman living in his house. But Paula assured him that Alexis was a sweetheart and completely trustworthy.

Rome also wasn't sure why his ex-wife was so trusting regarding him staying with her sister. He wasn't seeing anyone and wouldn't be responsible if something sexual happened given the circumstance. Rome looked at his phone and saw he had missed a buddy of his. He called Carlton back.

"Hey man. What's up," Rome asked.

"Hey you good. You on your way to get her," Carlton asked.

Carlton and Rome had spoken the night before and Rome had expressed reservations about the whole thing. "Yeah. Leaving in a minute. I swear I feel like this is some type of set up," Rome stated.

"Why you say that?" Carlton asked.

"I don't know. Just something about the way it went down," he replied. "Man, she just a control freak. She doesn't want no one around her son or you for that matter, and so she's sending her spy to watch your ass," Carlton said.

"We're divorced now, so she shouldn't be concerned with what I'm doing," he said.

"Yeah. You know how women are. She still wants to run shit. My thing is, you haven't even seen this sister. What if she's fine. I tried to look her up for you. I saw something on Facebook but the profile pic is a building and no posted pics except the same business pics on the company website. I looked up the website but it shows all different faces and two or more people in each picture. I couldn't tell if any of them was her. There was a really attractive, well dressed woman in one picture, standing with four other people. It was hard to say. You better hope it's not her. You going to have a hard time trying to keep from fucking if that was her," Carlton said.

Rome laughed. "She's not crazy. I know she wouldn't send a beautiful woman to my front door. We would definitely have a problem," he replied.

"Man, Paula is pretty. You think her sister's not gonna be at least kinda pretty. Yeah. Ok. Good luck with that one," Carlton joked.

"How will you know who she is?" Carlton asked.

"Paula told me she will have on all white, she's light brown and she's got long hair in a ponytail," he replied.

"What! She sounds fine already. What the fuck are you doing," Carlton joked. The two got off the phone and Rome called his mother Gladys to check up on Romy. Paula had already called both Rome and

Alexis to get their wardrobes to help them find one another. She also gave Alexis his number to call when she was in the terminal.

Alexis' plane touched down and she walked off and out into the terminal, immediately looking around for Rome. She had no picture and no idea what he would look like. She asked Paula to describe him and Paula told her he was handsome and would have on jeans and a black button-down shirt. She looked around, but saw no one matching that description. What she didn't know was he had already spotted her, and had stepped around the corner out of view.

"Carlton. Man. This is definitely going to be a problem," he remarked, as he paced the floor.

"I told you. Where she at now?" Carlton asked.

"Standing near the door with her bags, looking around," he replied.

"Ok. Keep your cool and just walk up to her. Try not to look at her like you want to tackle her and just play it cool," Carlton said.

Rome hung up the phone, gathered his composure then walked back into her view. Alexis was on her phone talking to Paula when she looked up.

"Paula. What the fuck. You said your husband was handsome. You did not say *fine*. What the fuck is wrong with you. He's coming my way," she said.

Paula smiled and looked over at Amy. "He's my ex and I did say fine. Anyway, call me when you get to the house," she said. Alexis sighed and hung up, as she tried not to blush.

"Hi. So, you're Rome," she said.

"Yes. You're Alexis," he asked.

"Yes," she said, trying not to blush. She was now more confused than ever. What was Paula thinking. Why had she made this request? Why would she put them together? It was obvious looking in his eyes that there was something there immediately. He tried to hide his attraction, but Alexis saw that he was. She would need to talk to Paula and soon. The sixty days would need to be cut down to two weeks and not a day longer.

Alexis and Rome walked through the airport and to his waiting SUV. Rome placed her bags in the back and got in. Alexis tried looking out the window and not at him. This was awkward and she needed to get a grip.

What the fuck is wrong with her. He is way to sexy for this shit. Damn! Penny would have his dick in her hand right this minute, she thought as she nervously sat next to him.

"So, you own a business," he asked, trying to make small talk.

"Um. Yeah. I have a design firm. I've only been in business a few years," she said smiling and continuing to look out into traffic.

Rome noticed her avoidance and smiled to himself. He also noticed that she was a beautiful flower. A sweetheart. Not the toxic monster Paula claim her sisters to be. She was sexy, alluring, sweet, polite and obviously successful based on the way she was dressed and the expensive Keepall bags she was carrying. He noticed everything about her and it dawned on him why Paula would probably keep him from her sister. But he was not the cheating type so he was back to square one. Why hide her and why reveal her now? He was ten steps ahead of her. Paula had some explaining to do.

When they pulled up to the house, Rome got out and grabbed Alexis' bags. She looked around in shock. She had no idea that her sister was living such a privileged life.

"This is a beautiful house," she said.

"Thanks," he replied, taking her bags up to the door. Paula's house looked like the smaller version of a castle with its unique shape and sophisticated charm. The landscaping looked like something out English Gardens magazine and was breathtaking.

Alexis followed Rome into the home and he showed her to her room. She was quiet and not saying much. He wasn't sure what to make of her mood change. She had talked, although choosing not to look his way, for the entire ride there. She had turned into a chatterbox and had told him everything about her business, their family and their other sister, Penny. Rome listened intently. Paula never told him anything. He knew absolutely nothing about their family and even less about the sisters.

"You ok," he asked.

"Oh yeah. Sorry," she said, grabbing her bag off the floor and placing it on the bed.

"Well, if you're ok, I'm going to run to my office," he said, staring at the back of her head waiting for her to look at him. She was looking down and trying not to give him any eye contact.

"Ok," she said.

Rome left out and she heard his car start up and ran to the window. Alexis watched as he pulled off and called Paula back.

"Hello," she answered.

"I can't do this Paula. The baby is nowhere around. It's just me and him, and he's sexy as fuck. What is going on? Why did you leave him? Tell me something that's gonna make sense cause right now I'm two seconds from getting on a plane," she stressed.

Paula sighed. "Ok. I'll tell you. But don't leave," she said.

Paula paused, took a deep breath and then told Alexis her secrets, her life's issues, the drama and why she left her beautiful home, her kid and fine ass man for London.

"I'm in love with someone else. Always was. He was someone I liked a lot and he was good for me. I never meant for things to go that far. I wasn't even trying to get pregnant. I was on the pill when I got pregnant with Romy. I wanted out. I realized my mistake, but it was too late. And now, I feel bad. Rome is busy and needs help. I can't come there. Not now. I just can't face him. And there's something else you don't know... I'm in love with a woman," she said. Alexis held the phone in shock. Paula held the phone knowing she needed to give Alexis a minute to absorb what she had just told her.

"What?" she replied. "Paula this is all too much. I can't talk right now. I need to go and call you back after I get unpacked and get comfortable. I will stay here for a few weeks, but I can't be here longer than that. I just can't," she said.

"It's ok if you're attracted to him. I don't care if you are. Whatever happens between you two, happens. I don't care. I'm not coming home Alexis. Do you get what I'm saying," she confessed.

"What?" Alexis said in a low voice, sitting down on the bed before she tumbled over from shock.

"Yes. I could care less if you fuck him or not. Just take care of my kid please," Paula replied.

Alexis looked at her phone. She couldn't believe the words that had just come out her sister's mouth. She had no reply. There was nothing to say. She needed to gather her composure. Replay the conversation. Try to understand what was going on under her own nose. Part of her wondered if he knew. Was this a plan. Alexis ended the call without a goodbye. She sat on the bed in a daze. She was frozen. She sat on the bed for a half hour just looking around, totally surprised by everything Paula had said.

So here she was, temporarily living in another city away from her office. Her sister had just revealed she was gay. Said she never loved her husband. Stated she left her child behind to chase behind some woman. And the cherry on top, was the fact that she was seriously attracted to her own sister's husband. Alexis shook her head. It was all too much. She grabbed her phone and called Penny and then walked over to the window to look out at the landscaping. She needed something serene to calm her.

"Hello," Penny answered.

"Pen. Are you sitting down?" she said, her voice filled with anxiety.

"No! What the fuck is up? Should I be on my way. I told you that bitch was crazy. I don't care that we're related. I will hurt her," she replied.

"Stop talking that way and listen. You're not going to believe what the fuck she just told me. Sit the fuck down and listen," she said.

"Ok Alexis. I'm sitting. What?" Penny replied.

"Paula said she's gay. Always was. Is moving to London to be with her woman. Wants me to stay here and help with her son and her husband...What the fuck...Ok... And the husband... the muthafucka is fine as all get out. Not the kind of man you can just walk past all day long. What the fuck..." she blurted.

Penny held the phone, her mouth wide open. The words took a minute to register.

"Are you fucking serious. Damn! She should have called me. Fine, rich and she don't want him. What the fuck. Told you the bitch is crazy," Penny replied.

"Don't call your sister that. What should I do?" Alexis asked.

"Alexis. You did not just ask me that. Are you asking what I would do or what *you* should do, cause that's two different answers," she said laughing.

"It's not funny Pen. This is serious," she stressed.

"Ok. Ok. You should stay, help with the baby and if you start catching feelings, fuck his brains out," she replied. Alexis chuckled but then shook her head. Penny was joking while she was being serious. She was in a real dilemma.

Alexis continued talking and looked down and saw her phone ringing with a number she did recognize. "Pen. I'll call you back. I'm getting a call," she said.

"Hello," she answered.

"Hey this is Rome. I was just checking on you," he said. Alexis' heart started pounding. He didn't have to say it was him. She would know that sexy voice anywhere.

"I'm ok," she said, pacing the floor and smiling uncontrollably.

"Ok. Well. I'll get there at seven. I have to get Romy first. I'll bring you something to eat. Anything you want in particular?" he said.

"No. Not really. Just bring anything," she said.

"Well there's a lot to snack on down in the fridge. And I'll bring you something later," he said.

"Ok," she replied. Alexis hung up the phone and shook her head. *This bitch is crazy!*

Chapter Seven – Attached

P

enny walked through her apartment door and slung her heels off. *I'm home. Yes!* she said, as she walked into her kitchen. She had a rough day. Meeting after meeting and to make matters worse, Tom was coming unglued.

He had started spiraling out of control after she received flowers from Camron. Tom knew she had other partners but Penny was more distant and was avoiding him and so he was becoming unpredictable. As she made her way to her bedroom her phone rang. *Damn!* Penny walked back toward her kitchen to grab her phone then sighed as she saw it was the fifth call from Tom. She sat her phone down and went back into her room. Penny ran herself a warm bath and got in and relaxed. She closed her eyes and immediately pictured Camron. The two had been seeing each other nonstop and she was ready to call off her fling with Tom.

She sat there several minutes, enjoying the warm water and relaxing. She washed her body and rinsed off and then sat for a few more minutes not ready to get out of the tub. As she leaned back to get more comfortable, she heard a knock at her door. *Dammit!* she said, as she grabbed her towel. Penny walked to her front door and looked out the peephole. *Fuck!* She opened her door slowly.

"You didn't see me calling you," Tom said, as he walked past her.

"Tom! What the fuck! You just come over. You don't wait to hear back from me. You don't own me," she said.

"Actually, I do," he replied. Penny gasped.

"You need to leave. Leave now Tom," she said. Tom sat down on her couch in defiance, refusing to leave.

Penny left him in the front room and retreated to her room to put her clothes on. Tom came in behind her and grabbed her tight. Penny struggled, as he forced her down on the bed. The more she struggled the harder he held her.

"So, you got a new man and now you forget all about me," he said.

"Tom... he stays here now. You have to leave before he gets here." Tom's eyes got big.

"He what? I pay the rent here!" he said.

"No! You used to pay the rent. He pays it now. Leave Tom." Penny heard the door open and jumped up. Tom stood up and Penny looked at him and shook her head, moving quickly passed him.

"Um Cam. It's not what you think. He was just leaving," she said, as Tom emerged from their bedroom looking heated and ready for a brawl. Camron looked at Tom and then back at Penny.

"What the fuck is going on? Who is that?" he asked.

"I'm the one who got her this place and the one who pays all the bills," Tom said.

Camron looked at Penny as he tried to calm himself. He was a lawyer. An up and coming powerhouse, and he didn't need any domestic issues on paper that involved him. Camron would have demolished Tom within seconds but decided against any the altercation. He was more mad at Penny, for putting him in the situation. Camron turned to leave and Penny tried to stop him.

"Where are you going? Don't leave," she cried. Camron pulled away and walked out, slamming the door and almost tearing it out of the frame.

"Get the fuck out Tom. I won't be in the office tomorrow or any other day. I no longer work there. You get out and don't fucking come back," she said, as she walked past him and slammed her bedroom door.

Tom stood motionless. He wasn't ready to leave. He still loved her and seeing her and her new lover, was difficult to take. Tom walked to the door. He thought about going into her room. But something told him she was over it. He exhaled sharply, his nose flaring. His stomach was in knots. It was really over. He had to face it.

R

ome finished up at the office and headed out. It was six o'clock and he had two stops to make. First, he needed to pick up food and second, he needed to get his son. He had a chef but his chef was on call and only worked when Rome scheduled him to.

Rome hadn't scheduled him and so there would be no one to cook unless he or Alexis cooked and he hadn't found out if she actually cooked yet. She had been there for two weeks and if she did cook, she hadn't done so yet. Rome stopped at his favorite Italian restaurant and grabbed two chicken pasta dishes and some chicken fingers and fries for Romy. He then headed to his mothers house to get his son.

"Hey ma," he said, as he walked past her.

"Hey hun. Romy is resting. He wore himself out and fell asleep right on my shaggy carpet in the den," she stated, laughing and walking behind her son following him into the den. Rome's mother was a classy, elegant woman who had raised five men. Two lawyers, a pharmacist, a doctor and her most accomplished son Rome who had a Masters in Technology and a Doctorate in Science. Gladys was herself an accomplished professor and taught at the prestigious Cornell University.

"Where's dad?" he asked.

"He was golfing with his buddies. Who knows. Probably went for drinks. He'll be here soon," she replied.

Gladys was only partially aware of her son and Paula's issues. He had told her they were divorcing but had refrained from giving her too much information. She never liked Paula and had warned him when he first brought her around that she sensed something and to avoid her. But Rome ignored his mother's advice and ended up regretting he did.

He knew he should have listened to her. She was the one woman who would never steer him wrong and she was usually right.

"So, what's going on with you? Paula coming back any time soon?" she asked.

"No. Not that I'm aware of. She's happy," he said.

"Oh. Well good for her. Just as long as she doesn't try to take my grandson, all is well," she said.

Gladys was happy Paula was gone. She didn't like the change in her son that was apparent after he had married her.

Gladys could tell Paula was playing mind games and she counted the days until she would be out. But then Paula became pregnant which didn't endear her to Gladys. It made Gladys more judgmental of her as she watched her daughter in law go from bad to worse with her neglect and selfish behavior.

Rome poured himself a glass of water and then went back in the den and picked Romy up. He was careful not to tell his mother about his new house guest. He knew how she felt about Paula and didn't want her prying or trying to talk him into sending Alexis back home because he had no plans of doing that anytime soon.

"Ok ma. I'll see you later. Thanks. You need anything?" he asked.

"No. I'm getting ready to fix myself a drink and watch my favorite show." she said, as she kissed her son bye.

Rome drove home making calls to his brother Nigel and his friend Carlton. He stopped at a liquor store and purchased red and white wine, vodka, tequila and scotch before he went in. He wasn't sure if she drank so he wanted to have liquor there for her. He and Paula didn't drink so he had a half-stocked bar meant for guests and he wasn't sure what was left. Romy had woken up during the ride and was back being active and playful. Rome pulled up and got Romy out of his car seat and walked in his house. It was quiet. Romy ran around as Rome walked through the house looking for Alexis. He peeked in her room but she was not there.

As he walked, he could hear her on her phone in his office. "Hey," he said, walking in.

"Hey. I hope you don't mind me on your computer. I was taking care of some business," she replied, hanging up on her phone call.

"No. Of course not," he said, as he turned and walked out. Alexis heard noises and smiled as she hurried to see her nephew.

"Hi Romy," she said, as the toddler stopped and stared at her. Romy hid behind his father leg then smiled as he ran away.

"He's a little shy," Rome said.

"He's ok. He'll come looking for me when he's ready," she said, as she turned and walked back into the office. Rome watched her walk back into the office. He liked the way she walked. She had sex appeal and it didn't go unnoticed.

A

lexis chuckled at her nephew. As predicted, he peeked in and she called him to her. "Come here Romy. Why are you being shy," she said, smiling at him. "Look what I got," she said, as she held up a piece of candy. Romy walked to her and she opened the candy from the wrapper and bit a piece off. She handed the much smaller piece to him and then popped the other half in her mouth. Romy did a dance as he delighted in the sweet flavors. Alexis was tickled. He was opening up to her. Romy stayed in the office and then ran to get a book and came back. "Oh. You want me to read this to you. Ok. Come on," she said, picking him up.

Alexis read to him and kissed his little cheek, as he started drifting back to sleep. Rome heard her reading to the baby and smiled as he walked back toward the kitchen. Romy fell asleep and Alexis held him as she tried to type with one hand. She made her way through her work and then shut the computer down. Just as she was about to get up, Rome walked in.

"Oh, he's asleep," he said, taking him from her.

Alexis handed him the baby and Rome told her that her food was in the kitchen. Alexis walked away as Rome watched her, fascinated with her body and turned on by her sultry presence. He knew he would have to battle his desires when he went to bed that night.

It had been a few weeks, and Alexis was becoming more comfortable at her sister's home. It had all the amenities a person could ask for and Rome and Romy were wonderful. She loved the baby and Rome was awesome. He went out of his way for her and she appreciated him. But she was attracted to him and was growing concerned. Alexis walked the gardens with Romy watching as he rode his bike down the path and into the small maze that Rome had designed for him to ride through. It was a huge zig zag design lined with shrubs with a beginning and an end so Romy wouldn't get lost.

Alexis stayed close, enjoying the breeze. She was nervous about her evening. Rome had asked her if she wanted to get out of the house. He suggested dinner and she said yes, but then learned that it would be just the two of them. Romy wouldn't be with them. He was going to his uncles for a sleepover with his cousins. And with his not there, Alexis worried about the dinner feeling like a date. She wondered what they would talk about and what they would do afterwards, without Romy there as a distraction.

After several hours, Alexis took the toddler inside and put him in the tub. She dressed him and then fed him and waited on Rome. Her and Romy sat in the front room, laid out across the couch watching cartoons and relaxing. Rome came home and kissed his son then followed him to the kitchen. He wanted another cookie and Rome wanted him happy so he would go without throwing a fit. "You'll be ready soon," he asked Alexis. "Yeah. I'm going to take a shower right quick. I should be ready by the time you get back from dropping him off," she said.

As evening approached, Rome prepared to drop his son off. "I'll be back soon. I was thinking we could go to this place called Madonna's. It's new," he said.

"Okay," Alexis said, as she bent down to tie her nephew's shoe. "I'll see you later okay. Be good," she said as she touched his cheek. Romy turned and ran to the door. Alexis chuckled then looked at Rome. He smiled back at her. His eyes staying on her a second longer than they should. Alexis looked away. She felt uncomfortable but couldn't cancel their evening out. She had dreamed of him just the night before and she hoped there was nothing in her eyes that gave her away.

The door opened and Alexis sat up. She heard him enter and she could hear his footsteps as he came down the hall. She took a deep breath. She had sat there and convinced herself that there was nothing but an innocent bond. They were family. And it was safe for her to eat with him. Paula would want her to. There was nothing going on. He was generous and sweet. He was also handsome and any woman would notice. She gave herself permission to go. She was in control of herself. Her dreams were just that. Dreams.

Rome walked into the family room. He could see Alexis had been sitting and waiting on him.

"You ready," he said, smiling at her.

"Umhmm," she replied, walking past him and going to his car.

Ok Alexis. Don't look nervous. You're just going to eat. This is not a date," she thought, as she opened the car door. Rome got in and started the car.

"I'm starved," he said as he pulled off.

"Yeah me too. Romy ran me all morning. Breakfast didn't hold me over. I'm ready to relax and eat something wonderful," she said.

Rome glanced over at her. She seemed to be somewhere else even though her lips were moving. He could pick up she was a nervous. He was too. He was falling for her and unsure how he was supposed to feel. Paula had all but abandoned her family and sent her beautiful, intelligent and sexy sister to stay with them and wasn't asking questions. And now his feelings were all but impossible to ignore even though he still had no compass for how to proceed.

They made small talk on the way to the restaurant. Rome told her about his day and the issues he had with one of his employees and how he ran two companies. Alexis took in every word. She liked the way his mind worked. He was intelligent, sophisticated and he had a heart. She could tell he really cared about his employees. The more he talked, the harder she fell. By the time they made it to the restaurant, forty minutes later she knew things would not be the same moving forward.

Rome did most of the talking as they sat and ate. Alexis ordered salmon and vegetables and Rome ordered ahi tuna and vegetables. Rome ordered their best white wine and hoped after a drink or two, Alexis would open up. She was a lot more talkative the first day she met him and seemed to get less talkative, the longer she was there. Alexis ate her food and sipped her wine. She knew not to drink more than one glass. She was a different person when she was tipsy and she didn't want to say or act in a way that came across as flirtatious.

"Can I ask you something," he said, looking at her with intensity. She sat her wine down and wiped her mouth with her napkin.

"Sure," she said, smiling to hide her unease.

"Are you seeing someone back in Atlanta," he asked. Alexis shook her head yes then followed up with a verbal yes.

She paused and Rome picked up his glass of wine and took a sip. The tension was thick and she decided to talk about it just a little and explain her situation. He was talking non-stop a minute ago and now he was silent.

"I was seeing someone. We broke up but then we slowly started seeing each other. I don't know what we're doing now," she said, as she picked up her wine and took another sip.

"Will you be staying longer?" he asked, trying to hide his disappointment, and trying to gage how much time he had to get her to stay.

"Yes. A little longer, I think," she said, sounding unsure. The two finished their meal and walked back to his car. Both were in an awkward position and neither had a clue what they were doing. All they knew was the obvious. That they liked each other.

Rome drove to work the next morning trying to get a grip. He had wanted to call Paula and try to get some an idea of what he was dealing with. Someone who could tell him about Alexis. He thought of how he could ask questions without being too forward. Get Paula talking so he could get answers without seeming to inquisitive. Alexis was keeping a distance but he could tell she was attracted to him. She was one big mystery to him and he had no one else to call. No one who knew her. He was afraid to come on strong, possibly pushing her away and back on a plane home.

As Rome wondered about her, he also wondered if this was Paula's plan all along. He had a feeling from day one, that there was more to the story other than she was sending her to be with Romy. He never told her he needed help with Romy. He was the one who practically raised the baby, tending to his ever need throughout their marriage. It seemed implausible that he would suddenly need help now.

Rome wanted to call her and confront her of his suspicions but he was afraid. Afraid that Paula may get jealous and then sabotage everything. But he took a chance and grabbed his phone and called her anyway.

"Hello," Paula answered. "Hey. I need to talk to you. Can you talk right now?" he asked. "Yeah I can. What's wrong?" she asked. "You tell me. I want you to be honest. Did you send her to me so I could be with her? Did you plan that?" he asked. Paula held the phone. She bit her nails. Her heart started to race. She did. But she was not prepared to admit it. It was a lot to admit.

"I wanted her to come there and help with Romy. But if you're asking me if I care if you fall in love with her and marry her, the answer is no," she replied. "That's not what I'm asking you. I want to know did you actually send her to me so that I would?" he asked, sounding serious. Paula held the phone again. Her long pause answered his burning question. Rome sighed as he waited for her to admit what he now suspected. That he was supposed to love Alexis. That she knew he would. And that she wanted them to be together. "Yes," she replied.

Rome sighed. "You didn't think you should have told me something like that?" he said, shaking his head and rubbing his goatee. "Why are you asking me this now. She's been there for a few weeks now. Has something happened?" she asked. "Yeah something has. I'm falling for her and she seems to be having a hard time adjusting. She avoids me," he said, sounding frustrated. "Have you told her how you feel? Tell her Rome. Don't tell me. Tell her. I have to go. I'll call you when Amy leaves. I can't talk in front of her."

"Come on Pebbles pick up," Penny said, as she drove back home from her grocery store run. Her life was in shambles and she needed to talk to her sister. This was the exact reason she didn't want her to leave. She feared this very thing. Needing her and not being able to reach her. Alexis had fallen asleep with Romy laying right next to her after a day at the park, while Rome was at his office. *Damn!* she said, as she hung up. She decided to send a text that read:

Call me. Everything has fallen apart. Camron came home and Tom was there and now he won't call me. I had to quit TNT behind all this shit and now I'm living off my savings until something else comes up. I need to talk to you. Call me as soon as you can.

Penny parked in her spot and carried her groceries in. She put them away then plopped down on her couch. She turned on her tv and grabbed her throw and laid there drifting off when her phone rang with a return call from Alexis.

"Alexis. Where the hell have you been. First off mom is worried about you she said call her, she hasn't talked to you in a few days. What's going on? You tell me first because I got so much to tell you it's going to take five hours, so you first," she said, eagerly waiting on an update. She had hoped Alexis would say she had fucked Rome but no such luck.

"Nothing really. I was supposed to come home yesterday. I've been here for weeks now and I promised myself I would come home but I'm not ready to leave," she said.

"Oh yeah. And why not? Gone and say it. I'll tell you why. I can hear it in your voice," Penny said.

"Shut up. You think you know everything," she replied.

"No. But I know that sound. I know when a woman has fallen in love. She sounded just like you sound now. If that's not it, then why are you still there? Have you slept with him yet? Please tell me you at least fucked him?" she asked.

"Damn Penny, no! Everything is not about sex. Ok," she replied.

"Oh shit bitch. Hold up. You mean to tell me that you gone over him and you haven't sampled the dick yet. You might as well close Alexis Allen Designs down. Your ass is not coming back and if you moving there, so am I," Penny cautioned.

"I'm trying to keep it cordial but I ain't doing so well. I want him bad. I didn't see this happening," she said,

"Never mind me what happened with Camron?" she asked.

"Oh Pebs. Everything is so fucked up. Camron left," she said, as she burst into tears.

"Don't cry Pen. He'll be back. He's just mad. What happened?" she said, worried about her big sister.

"Tom brought his dumb ass over here and fucked everything up. He did that shit on purpose. He knew I was pulling away from him. He just showed up. And Camron came home saw him and left," she stated, as she cried.

"Ok. First of all. I'm shocked you like him enough to cry over him. And second, since when have you ever thrown the towel in so fast. You know he's coming back. He's somewhere now, jacking off, trying to figure out how he's gonna get back in your good graces and not look like a punk while doing so. He needs to be a man and better yet look like one. He feels punked out. Just wait. You'll see," Alexis assured. "That's why you need to come home. I'm a tough bitch when you're here."

Alexis smiled and then took the phone away from her ear when she heard the door close. "Pen. He's here. I'll call you back," she said. "Ok Alexis. But fuck him. Please. Fuck him for me. Just do it," she said, as they giggled and got off the phone. Alexis wasn't ready for that. She saw the way he looked at her and she knew he wanted her. But she wasn't sexually aggressive enough to open that door so she laid there and closed her eyes. Rome came into her room and stared at her. She kept her eyes closed as he watched her laying there. He walked around to the other side of the bed and picked his son up and left out, closing the door slowly behind him.

Alexis grabbed her phone and texted; *He stood here staring at me. He was watching me. This is getting deep. I'm not in control of my feelings anymore. And I'm worried about the aftermath. Like, what happens afterwards. Like. What if I fall in love with him? Like, really in love. Is this just a possible fling to him?*

Penny replied; *The way you describe him he doesn't seem like the fling type. He's probably in love now and just hasn't said anything. If you not ready for all that then maybe you should come home.*

Chapter Eight – Home Bound

P

aula looked at her phone and noticed she had several missed calls from Alexis. She sat her phone down and took a couple of deep breaths. She had a feeling what the calls were about. Amy wasn't home so she had the privacy she needed to make the difficult call.

She had already talked to Rome and so she decided to call Alexis and just get it over with. Alexis obviously had more to say and she would need to come clean. She wanted to come clean so that Alexis could stop feeling guilty about liking Rome. Paula called Alexis and got nervous when she answered. She didn't know how Alexis would handle was she was about to say to her.

"Hey," Alexis answered, sounding glad to hear from Paula. She had tried her a few days earlier too but got no answer.

"Hey. How's everything?' Paula asked.

"I don't know. I have feelings for him. I know you said you don't care if I sleep with him but it's more than that and I didn't come here for that. I can't believe you just walked away from him. I mean, I don't get that," she said, sounding frustrated at her own fears and desires. She sounded like a woman in love and Paula had something to say.

The thing is I have been seeing her the whole time. I am in love and have always loved her. Only her. I never loved him. When I met him, he came on strong and he pursued me and he was hard to say no to. I wasn't ready to be open about liking women, so I tried to make it work but I couldn't. Then I started feeling guilty. He seemed to be content with me just being there and that seemed to work for a while. Until I cut him off sexually and then he became distant. I had hoped he would find someone and make things easier, but he kept wanting to work it out. But the more he pushed, the more I resisted and I started being with Amy even more. I was too embarrassed to tell him and I wasn't ready to say I loved a woman so I tried to keep everything under wraps. But not anymore. I am moving here. With her. I want him to send Romy here for visits. I know he won't let Romy live with me in a different country. So, I'm fine with visitation. We already worked out everything. We split the money. Will get a divorce eventually. There was plenty of money, so I didn't care. I had my own. Amy has money. He has money. Money was not the issue, she confessed.

"Ok... So why involve me?" Alexis asked, upset at the realization that this was planned. That Paula had planned for her to fall in love with Rome.

"I wanted you to be with him and help him raise my son. I don't trust him to pick someone who will love my son. I knew you would be attracted to him and I know he can help you with your company. He can give you what you need to turn it into a large company. He is a master at building companies up. You can't lose with him," Paula stated, holding the phone.

Alexis remained silent as she weighed her words. She loved her sister but this side of her sister was unknown to her. Penny would have never made a plan that involved choosing the direction her life would go and not tell her. Penny would never have even made the attempt. "Paula. I'll stay for a little while, then I'm going home."

"What the hell..." Alexis said, still in shock, as she walked through the massive empty home. It was inconceivable that her sister would have done such a thing. Yes, her life was admirable. Yes, she had an adorable child and a husband any woman would want to be with. It didn't help that she felt at home. The house, so impressive, that even the wealthy would take notice. It was a perfect life.

But Paula had gone too far. Her plot to hook her up with Rome, was more than she could bear. He was extremely attractive and she noticed the chemistry between them immediately, but he was Paula's husband. Not even her ex. No papers filed. No notice given. Nothing. She simply hopped on a plane to another country. She had simply left, hoping Alexis would pick up the pieces.

Alexis couldn't understand her sister. Who would leave such an adorable son and such a handsome, smart and sophisticated husband. Paula never did follow any rules. She always did what she wanted, when she wanted. And Alexis and Penny where always there to pick up the pieces. Alexis stared out the window. Her breath leaving steam on the glass. She looked at her vague reflection. She knew she was already going down the road of no return. She was already intrigued with Rome. Already wondering about him. Wanting him. Turned on by him. *I have to leave soon. Or I won't want to!*

"Hey. Anybody here," Rome yelled. Alexis emerged from the kitchen. "Hey. How was work?" she asked. "Good," Rome replied, smiling and admiring the woman she was. Alexis was nothing like Paula. Paula hired cooks and housekeepers to take care of things. Alexis preferred to do things on her own. Even after repeated request and suggestions from Rome, Alexis chose to do all the cooking and most of the cleaning. The size of the house left her with no choice but to hire a cleaning service.

"Where's Romy?' he asked. "Oh! He's asleep. He fell out as soon as we got here," she replied. Alexis walked away as Rome watched her walk. His eyes scanned her backside and his mind raced. Alexis was shapely and the stretch jeans and small fitted black tee fit her curves perfectly. Rome liked women who dressed more corporate. Slacks, skirts and blouses were his preference, but not anymore. Alexis had him fixated on jeans and tee shirts. She had a way of wearing casual clothes with flair and sophistication that oozed sex appeal.

"You hungry. I made lobster penne and garlic bread. I know how much you love lobster," she said. Rome walked into the kitchen and over to the stove.

"Wow. That smells good," he said. Alexis looked up at him. He stood a few inches over her at 5'11.

"Did you eat yet?" he asked.

"No. I was waiting on you," she said, as she picked up her spoon. Rome stared at the back of her head. He wanted to kiss her, but he was unsure she would be receptive. Alexis kept her eyes on her food. Stirring the pot as she tried to get the sauce to spread more evenly. She could feel his breath on her. He stood close. She became nervous. The tension was thick.

"Will you eat down here with me," he asked.

"Sure," she said.

Alexis had been retreating to her room with her plate while Rome ate with Romy. Sometimes the baby would follow her and eat with her in her room. Rome knew she was still uncomfortable so he never asked. But this day he wanted her to. He hoped she would start eating with him. He understood their situation was an uncomfortable one, but he wanted to be around her. He couldn't help it and it wasn't either one of their faults.

"Pen... What the hell! I told you his ass was crazy, but you wouldn't listen," Alexis said, as she paced her bedroom in nothing but thong panties. Rome heard her conversation and stopped to listen. He liked her laughter. The way she chuckled. He stood outside her bedroom door. Alexis had neglected to close it completely and left the door slightly ajar.

Rome pushed on the door slowly, hoping not to startle her, or disrupt her conversation. He wanted to ask her if she would accompany him to a dinner at a new prestigious school called Creative Arts Institute. It was a dinner honoring business owners' who had made contributions to their private school.

Rome stood at the doorway. Alexis came from behind the closet door, her attention completely on her phone call. Rome quickly turned his head when he saw she was naked with nothing on but panties. He started to walk away but then turned back around and continued watching. She was beautiful. Breathtaking. Her carefree spirit shinning.

"Why would you do that? See that's your problem. You fucked the man and now he's gone mad. Didn't we talk about this," Alexis said, smiling as she looked at herself in the mirror. She opened a jar of Vaseline and scooped out a large amount. She rubbed it on her arms and around her chest and shoulders. She scooped out another hand full and rubbed it on her breast and slowly down her stomach as she giggled at the ramblings of her promiscuous sister and her men problems.

As she rubbed her body something caught her attention. Alexis looked and was startled. She stared at Rome in the mirror, never turning around to him. She held the phone stunned, as his eyes peered through hers. Her hands seemed to move in slow motion. She wasn't sure what to do. He was looking at her naked. Watching her. The sight of him stealing a look turned her on. Alexis looked down and scooped more Vaseline out and then looked back to the door. She shook her head. He was gone.

"Pen! Oh my god. He saw me! He saw me naked," she whispered.

"Good, cause I'm sick of it. Paula don't want him. You'll see. He'll tell you soon enough," Penny replied.

"Shut up. I can't just get with him. Just like that. Anyway, I have to go. He probably wanted something," Alexis said.

"Yeah, he wants you," Penny replied.

"Shut up! Love you! I gotta go. I'll talk to you later."

Alexis put on her robe and walked out and down the hall. She looked around. She wondered where he'd gone. The house was eerily quiet as though he had left. Soon there was the sound of a cell phone ringing and Alexis walked in the direction of the sound, towards the family room.

"Hey. Did you want something?" she asked, looking shy and slightly embarrassed, as she approached him. Rome looked embarrassed himself, but quickly gathered himself and tried to appear unfazed.

"Um. Yeah. Sorry! I know this is last minute but I wanted you to accompany me to this function. My mother's not ready to release Romy yet. She wants to keep him all night. So, it works out cause there's this dinner tonight. I had two tickets and um... Hey listen. Um...Sorry I entered unannounced. I was coming to ask you. But then I just..." he said.

Alexis smiled. He looked embarrassed at being caught watching her. She felt bad for him. But the truth was she liked him watching. She started to cover her breast at first but didn't. She wasn't sure why she didn't.

"It's okay. I was taking forever to put some clothes on running my mouth with my sister. Yeah. That's sound wonderful. I haven't been to a dinner like that in a long time," she replied, looking intensely at him. The tension thick enough to cut. Rome smiled. His eyes matched her intensity. He was excited they were going. He usually passed on functions unless it was for a great cause. He was usually too busy and Paula usually went in his absence. "I'll go get ready," she said.

"I said nine," Rome complained to the company he usually hired whenever he needed a limo. He was nervous since eight thirty was approaching and he still had no driver.

"I'm sorry Mr. Wade. The driver is on his way. He said he's stuck in traffic," the man said.

"He'd better be here. Or you'll never take me or my family anywhere ever again," he complained.

Rome glanced to the top of the stairs then back to the window. Alexis would be emerging at any moment. She had been getting ready for a while. She had raided Paula's closet and found a red backless dress with the tags still attached. Besides Paula's breast being bigger than hers and her ass being bigger than Paula's their dress size was the same.

Rome hung up and sighed. This was a special night for him. A chance to be with Alexis. Someone he had grown fond of. Someone he admired. Someone he saw himself with. Rome had a lot of female suitors who had secretly admired him from afar but Alexis was his only desire. The only woman he wanted. Even Paula didn't stand a chance.

Rome heard Alexis' bedroom door open and watched as she emerged looking breathtaking. His eyes fixed on her as she slowly descended the staircase.

"Wow. You look beautiful," he said.

"Thank you," Alexis said, as she walked up to him.

"I need you to fasten the top button," she said, as she turned around. Rome was nervous. She smelled like a bouquet of flowers mixed with vanilla. Her smell alone had him on edge. He moved her hair over and began buttoning the remaining one she couldn't reach.

Alexis got chill bumps at his tender and careful touch. His breath once again on her skin. His cologne sexy and magnetic. She noted the smell. It brought back memories. It was the cologne he had on when he first came to get her from the airport. Alexis chuckled. He seemed to be taking too long for three buttons.

"What are you doing," she laughed.

"What. This fabric is thin. I don't want to tear it," he said.

"You won't," she laughed.

"There," he said, as he fastened the last one.

"They here yet ?" she asked.

"No."

Alexis walked away and into the kitchen. She grabbed a bottle of water and walked back into the great room. "I think this him here," Rome said, as he walked towards the door. Alexis watched him as he walked towards the door. She liked watching him whenever he was otherwise too busy to notice. She tried not to be obvious, but he was the sexiest man she had ever seen. She thought again about her sister and how she could possibly not want her life. A fabulous life. Filled with things, family, possibilities and the love of a great man. Rome was a strong and confident man. Loyal. Home every night. Brilliant. And an awesome father.

"You ready," he said, slightly startling Alexis and causing her to come out of her daydream.

"Huh. Oh," she said, as she grabbed her clutch and walked out the door. Rome followed her, locking up and walking side by side with her to their awaiting limo.

R

ome helped Alexis out of the limo and the two walked into the prestigious and impressive center. Spot lights flashed in the sky as dozens of people piled into the large hall with massive ceilings and chandeliers throughout. The hall was attached to the school and its grand opening was weeks away. The ceremony included, guest speakers, a live band and several students there to sketch renderings of the guest.

Alexis was greeted by a young lady who offered to take the shawl she had on her arm. Alexis carried it in case she got cold. "No thanks," she replied, as she tensely looked around. Rome stopped to talk to a small gathering of men and women he knew. He excused himself and smiled at Alexis then walked over to them. She smiled then became uncomfortable as she stood a few feet away from him. Soon Rome motioned for her to come over. Alexis gather her composure then walked over. She instantly had visions of the group being friends of Rome and Paula's and she wasn't sure how she felt about meeting anyone. She had hoped they would stick together, stay a minute then leave.

"Well hello gorgeous," one of the gentlemen said. His eagerness at meeting Alexis had Rome feeling possessive of her.

"Alexis this is Thomas Warren. And these are old friends of mine, Jerry Bradley and Steve Hines," He said, introducing the men. Alexis smiled and shook each man's hand.

"Nice to meet you," she said. Rome placed his hand on Alexis back and then looked at his friends.

"I'll talk to you later. We just got here. I need to find my table. Get her comfortable," Rome said.

Alexis immediately noted his touch. She noticed that he said the word "we" and that he stated he wanted her comfortable. His attention had her proud. Alexis believed that a man should always make a woman feel comfortable and so his efforts were noted. He had endeared himself to her, effortlessly. Just the gesture had her looking at him in a more romantic way which made her uneasy.

Alexis became more comfortable at the party, moving around and talking to several of Rome's friends as he looked on. Rome tried to do so, discreetly, but was caught several times by Alexis. She grinned at him and continued her conversation, slowly walking around and taking in the scenery. Rome excused himself and walked up behind her.

"You seen enough?" he asked. Alexis turned to him.

"No! You ready to go?" she asked.

"No... I was just wondering," he asked.

"I see how much fun you're having with your friends. Go ahead. It's nice here. The food is good. And I'm wasn't finished with my drink. I'm good," she replied with a light chuckle. Rome kissed her on the cheek and walked away.

Ok bitch! You're in trouble! she thought.

"Hey! You are... Alexis right," the man said. Alexis blushed then looked around for Rome. It was an instinct and she caught herself. She wasn't sure why she was concerned. Why she worried.

"Yes I am," she replied, still scanning the crowd.

"So, Rome says you're his wife's sister. That was nice of you to be his escort for the evening with Paula gone and all," he said, smiling and hoping Alexis would fill in the rest. The revelation made her feel some sort of way. She wasn't sure, but she was immediately bothered by the way her presence was described.

"Yes. Well..." she said, as she counted the seconds until he would leave. She was now ready to go.

"He said you're single. Is that true?" he said, causing her mood to shift. She was now angered. Even more, she was humiliated.

Alexis was unsure why she felt humiliated. Unsure why she was jealous. Why she didn't want to be looked at, as accompanying him. "So, are you married?" he asked. Alexis scanned the crowd once more. Furious but doing a great job at hiding it.

"No," she said, as she tried to give him what little attention she could. The truth was she was growing anxious by the second.

"Listen. So, while you're in town, can I show you around?" he asked.

"What?" Alexis said, in a *matter of fact* way which made the man pause.

"I just wanted to show you around. Show you the city," he said, hoping for a chance with her. He had watched her all evening and hoped she was single. Just then Alexis saw Rome as he was consumed in his conversation with a young lady. Rome looked up and then immediately walked over to her. He saw Steven standing with her and moved quickly to get to them.

"Hey," he said, as he approached. The vibe he got from Alexis cooled his spirit. "Everything ok?" Rome asked. "Yeah. I'm going to go to the ladies' room," she said, as she turned and walked away. Alexis felt herself becoming emotional and she was mad at herself for not having more control. A fear of him being able to see her emotions, had her hastily make her exit. Rome stared at her as she walked down the hall towards the restrooms.

"What's wrong with her? Did you say something to her?" Rome asked. He knew his friend Steve. Tact and respect were not at the top of his list of traits.

"Nothing man. What do you mean? I thought that was your sister-in-law," he said.

"Yeah, she is. But that doesn't mean you get to disrespect her," Rome said, his voice carrying with it a hint of anger.

"Wait! What! Who said I disrespected anybody? I just asked her if I could take her around. Show her the city," he replied.

Rome looked at him, unable to hide the jealousy he felt. A look that took Steve by surprise. "No! You can't," Rome said, as he walked away. Steve shook his head. He had known Rome for over ten years. They had never had words. His harsh *no* and abrupt departure, were familiar behavior. It spoke of a man involved.

Rome stood outside the women's restroom for what felt like a century. He paced slowly, constantly looking at the door. He managed a half smile as women looked at him before they entered. The restroom was down a otherwise lonely hall away from the party area. After several minutes Alexis emerged. "You ok?" he asked. Alexis wasn't alright but she didn't feel she had a right to feel any of the feelings she was feeling. "I'm ok. Can we leave soon?" she asked.

Rome hesitated. She had just stated she didn't want to leave. Just an hour prior, she had told him she wasn't ready to go. "What's wrong Alexis?" he asked, sincerely wishing she would open up and be honest with him. If she would reveal anything, they would embark on the love affair. He was ready. He wanted her. But she was Paula's sister. This was her call. "I'm just ready to go Rome. Please," she said, as she walked away.

S everal more weeks had gone by since the night at the black tie affair. Alexis was being strangely quiet at first but was back to being her usual self. The ride home that night was awkward for them. Rome believed Steve had said something that pissed Alexis off. But something deep down told him Steve had said something she didn't like about them. He had no filter, and Rome hoped he hadn't approached her. If he had, it would have been out of place. Rome wanted that night far behind them. His affections for her was becoming something he wasn't sure he could control. And the last thing he wanted was interference from someone like Steve.

Rome took a shower and lounged afterwards while Alexis gave Romy a bath. He was ready to get Alexis and Romy out of the house. He had been working overtime and had planned a day out. Rome had made a few runs in the morning but made sure to be back home early. He was taking his son to the show to see a cartoon and he wanted Alexis to go even though he had not said anything to her yet.

They had been having nice family dinners together and Rome wanted to make up for the evening at the center. Rome was bringing carry out home most evenings. He wanted Alexis to relax. He felt she was under too much pressure. And he was afraid he would lose her. He hadn't figured out how he was going to ask her that he wanted her to stay. And so, he wanted her life made easy.

But Alexis had started cooking every night again, instead of eating carry outs. She could only do so much of the carry out food and had started making everyone home cooked meals. Rome was surprised. He was glad she preferred to feed them. It felt like a wife to him. And he liked the feeling. He loved her cooking anyway. She cooked just as good as his chef and so he hadn't seen his chef in weeks.

Rome got a call that he needed to sign some papers so he ran to his office and returned an hour later. He returned home and walked in the door. He was immediately greeted by his son who hadn't seen him yet since he woke late. Romy immediately ran up to him, "Daddy," he said, as he grabbed his leg. "Hey man. Where's Alexis?" he said. Romy pointed to the front room and Rome walked in, with Romy running past him and jumping in Alexis arms. It was obvious to Rome that his son had completely bonded with Alexis and was comfortable around her. He saw her on the new laptop he ordered for her and surprised her with.

"Hey. You Ok?" he asked. "Yeah. Just looking at something on my website," Alexis said, closing it so she could play with Romy. "I was thinking we could go to the show today," he said. Alexis smiled at him.

"Yeah. That sounds like fun," she said, as she kissed Romy and played with him. Alexis looked up showtimes and selected a time a few hours away and continued on her laptop. Rome came and sat down near her feet.

"What time we going?" he asked. Alexis thought for a minute. "I selected the three o'clock time," she replied. Rome sat there with her going through his phone. Alexis peeked up and watched him. She loved the way he was and she loved the attention he seemed to be showering her with. He went out of his way to be in the same room she was in as big as the house was. It was a noted sign of his growing affections. And she was torn over her own growing feelings for him.

She smiled and continued typing in the description of a new line of chairs she would be showcasing. She had talked to Delano, while Rome was at work, and he told her he ordered the chairs as she instructed. Alexis never called Delano in front of Rome. She instinctively just avoided it. She had told him about Delano and how his sales skills helped build her company and he was quiet the next day as if secretly mad at her. She felt as though she was in a relationship that hadn't been made known yet, not even to her.

It was three o'clock and the movie would be starting soon. Rome Alexis and Romy loaded in the SUV headed for the theater. They parked in a parking deck and walked through and made their way up the escalator and into the show lobby. Alexis retrieved the tickets while Rome stood in the food line with Romy. Alexis looked over and saw two women whispering. They stared at Rome and she smiled. She had watched as other women flirted with him before when they went to the park and to another show but this time was different. She felt jealous. Her jealousy increased when she saw the women speak to him. And even more, when he laughed and talked with them.

He looked over at Alexis and she looked away. She tried not to be affected by it and filled the cups with soda and took her time grabbing condiments and napkins, putting them in her purse. She realized that women would always be attracted to him. It was something they both had to deal with because men blatantly flirted with her if Rome was not standing right next to her. After getting their snacks, they went into the theater and sat down and watched the movie and left after a few hours.

Rome noticed she was not into the movie and appeared distant. He wondered if she was feeling some sort of way because of his attention towards the women in the lobby. He watched her off and on throughout the movie but she kept her attention to the screen. He was sure she was purposely keeping her eyes from his. Concern grew. Tension increased until it was thick enough to slice. Rome sighed. He needed to make things right. No sooner than the thought crossed his mind, other thoughts tried to make sense of what he was feeling.

If she's mad then that means she cares. What are we doing? I'm falling in love with her. And I don't care anymore. I love this woman! But what do I say? What is she doesn't feel the same? But why else would she be mad. This is crazy! I still don't care!

Rome drove home and looked over. Alexis and Romy had fallen asleep. He stared at her as the car sat idling at a red light. He wanted to kiss her. Touch her face and tell her how he felt. It was words he was sure would flow with ease. He had never felt so complete. No woman had ever filled him with such warmth and happiness. He wondered how he would ever get by without her.

She was the missing link. His other half. It was a feeling he never felt with Paula. Guilt had been replaced with true love. There was nothing he could do now except find a way. Words and honesty could be the start of the greatest love affair or rip a family apart. A sister bond could be destroyed for good. Rome rubbed his goatee as he pulled off and headed for the expressway. He glanced over once more. She looked beautiful. Peaceful. He wanted Alexis bad. He just wasn't ready to say anything. Not yet. He needed more time. He had to be sure.

T

he next several days Rome spent at home playing with his son and spending time with Alexis. He taught her how to play chess and took her to a chess tournament. It was a hobby he relished in. He was a master player himself. And Alexis was impressed. He was the smartest man she'd ever met. He was incredible.

"How long you been playing," Alexis asked as she sat across from him trying to decide her next move. As she went for one of the Pawns, he shook his head no and smiled at her.

"No. Ok. Wait," she said, as she looked at what she had left. "This one?" she asked.

"No. If you move that one, what will happen? You don't see my position," he said, looking keenly into her eyes.

Alexis looked on the board and scanned each man carefully as Rome looked at his phone. His brother texted him, reminding him of the small get together he was having that next evening. As he texted back, Romy ran into the room and jumped in Alexis' lap. "I think he's tired. I'll put him in bed. And finish beating you in chess later," she said, smiling as she walked away.

Rome texted his brother then got up and walked into the kitchen and grabbed a bottle of water and headed to his room. As he walked by Romy's room, he stopped and listened as Alexis read to him. He continued walking and went into his room and cut on the tv. Rome dozed off for a minute then awoke and walked through the house toward Alexis' room. As he passed Romy's room, he peeked in but continued on to Alexis' room. He walked in and heard the shower going and stood there listening to her hum a song as she showered. He smiled at how soft and lovely her voice was. He wanted her. He wanted to get undressed and get in the shower with her.

As he stood there fantasizing about Alexis, the shower cut off abruptly. He panicked and then walked back slowly. He turned around and looked back and saw Alexis emerge from the shower. He stopped and stared at her in awe as she slowly dried her body off. Her bedroom was dark and she didn't see him standing their watching her. Her body had him in a physical dilemma. His penis instantly became rock hard for something he wanted and couldn't have. Her curvy figure with breast that sat up perfect and beautiful soft skin was enough to ejaculate to. She was visual perfection. He was shocked that she shaved her vagina completely bald and felt his dick get instantly hard from the sight of it. He backed out of the room slowly, wanting to watch her for much longer but afraid of being caught. She was beautiful. Stunning. His dream girl.

Rome left out and went into his room and shut the door. He got back in bed and laid there with nothing on his mind except Alexis who was in the next room and naked. He wished he could go back and kiss her. He wanted to tell her that he was in love with her and make love throughout the night. But he wondered if he wasn't alone in his feelings. She seemed fond of him. The way she hung on his every word. The way she smiled at him. The way she appeared to innocently flirt with him at times. He had to find out. He didn't know what her plans were but he hoped they involved him. He hoped against all odds that she loved him too.

The next evening Rome and Alexis went to his brothers cook-out after they dropped Romy off to his grandmother's house. "Hi. Welcome," Nigel's wife greeted as they walked in. Rome introduced Alexis to everyone and watched as Alexis made herself at home talking to several of the people there and appearing comfortable and relaxed. She would occasionally scan the room looking for Rome who watched as she looked for him. He would look away when she located him, then go back to staring at her.

Their game of innocent yet longing stares was building on tension that was becoming harder to hide. Alexis watched Rome often and closely then looked away if she saw his eyes scan the room. It was obvious to Nigel and his wife that the two had strong feelings for each other. They both continually checked for the other no matter who they were talking to or what they were doing.

"So, what's up man," Nigel said, as he approached his brother. "Nothing much. How's work," Rome asked. "Good. Won that last case I told you about. It's all good," he replied. "So, what's up with you and her? You tell her how you feel?" Nigel asked, looking at his brother. "What you mean," he replied. "You know. I know you. You in love with her. It's all in your face. You seem happy. You didn't seem this happy when you were with Paula. Not even in the beginning. Even mom notices," he said.

Rome looked around. He wasn't ready to admit anything. He was afraid of being judged by his brother's strict and rigid values. "I don't know man. It's nothing. I mean. She's beautiful. Who wouldn't fall in love with her. You know what I mean. But we're not together. She's just here to help with Romy," he replied. Rome tried to appear unfazed by her presence in his life. His family was traditional. Judgmental. They liked things to appear perfect.

But of all the family members he could have opened up to, it would have been Nigel. He was the least judgmental. He had his own improper indecencies and he knew what it was like to love a woman when all the rules say you shouldn't. But his brother playing coy didn't fool him. Nigel didn't believe a word of it. He knew Rome better than he thought and Nigel didn't miss much when it came to his family. He was an extremely perceptive man and noticed the smallest of details. "Tell her man. Tell her how you feel. I'll bet she surprise you. She probably feels the same."

Chapter Nine – Crumbling Walls

P

enny tried to get over Camron by spending her days going through the job postings and checking her emails for jobs in her area that matched her qualifications. She had money saved so she wasn't pressed for something immediately, but she did want to get back in the workforce. She bored easily so she wanted to earn income but she also needed the job as an outlet.

She put her reading glasses on and looked through a local magazine that had a job postings section at the end. Leah had suggested looking there as she stated she had found a few good listings there. Penny looked through the ads and then suddenly heard her door handle turning. She looked up and Camron was walking in. Penny tried to play tough and keep her cool.

"Your bag is packed and in the room, if that's what you're here for. I don't know why you left it behind in the first place," she said, looking at the magazine and refusing to look up at him. "Oh yeah," he said, as he stood there. Penny looked up at him and back at her magazine.

"You look sexy in those glasses. I always liked you in glasses. You look like a sexy school teacher," he said, as he walked over to her. "Don't touch me Camron. I don't know where you been. You think you can just leave when you get ready. Pop back up anytime. It doesn't work that way," she said, looking at him and trying not to show how badly she missed him. Camron pulled her up out of the chair and picked her up.

He put her down on the same spot on the counter he had when they first met and started to kiss her.

Penny took her glasses off and threw them and kissed him passionately as they both moaned. "I missed you baby," he said, as he kissed her and opened up her robe and saw she had nothing on underneath. "You must of knew daddy was coming home today," he said. Penny laughed and pulled him closer to her. She got down off the counter and got on her knees.

"You better had come back. A few more days and I was coming looking for you," she replied, as she stuck his entire penis in her mouth. Camron almost pulled a patch of her hair out as he grabbed her hair and pumped her mouth. He was so excited that she had to pull back and tell him to take it easy. But Penny was to skilled for him and he came in her mouth before she even pulled out her bags of tricks on him. Camron pulled her up and said, "I'm not done. Go in the room."

Penny walked slowly to the room teasing him as he followed behind her. One they got to her room, he bent her over the bed. She laid just her head on her bed, keeping her legs on the floor and he entered her from behind and fucked her for a half hour with no break. He was venting and told her that if he ever came home to a man in his house, he would not be so nice. "Bring somebody else up in here Penny and we going to have a serious problem."

Penny and Camron spent days under each other, barely coming up for air. They had missed one another and spent several days hanging out and spending quality time indoors. He made a few calls and got Penny interviews but she didn't like what her job duties entailed and so she didn't take any of the positions offered to her. Camron told her to take her time.

He made enough to cover her expenses and Penny slowed down her efforts. She never told Camron that Tom had called her asking her to come back to TNT which she politely turned down. Penny knew better than to get into his clutches.

"Damn. I wonder what Alexis is doing. I haven't talked to her in a few days. The last time I talked to her she sounded different. She's falling for him," she said, looking at Camron.

"That's ok baby. You want her to be happy. Right," he replied. "Yeah but that's not it. She sounded different in a bad way, not a good way. Like she had a lot on her mind. And she wouldn't tell me, which is not like her."

R

ome had a busy day planned. He had meetings with his staff at both of his businesses. It was his quarterly meetings that he had at both Fusion Marketing and Impact Digital. He had been on the phone all morning making sure that the PowerPoints and flow charts were ready at both locations. He had the best secretaries in the city.

Both Erin and Tanasha were skilled at all levels of information gathering and presentation. They had both been employed with him for years and knew how he liked to present and what he needed for his meetings. Alexis was totally unaware of these important meeting when she called him to tell him she was leaving. Rome was on his cell phone driving through traffic after dropping Romy off to visit with his grandmother when his phone rang. "He looked at the caller id and saw Alexis' name and clicked over without saying anything to who he was speaking to.

"Hello," he said, anxious to see what she wanted. She never called him and the only other time he looked on his phone and saw anything come in with her name was a few texts telling him to bring milk home for Romy or whatever else they needed. "Hello," she said, stressed and nervous about the call.

"Hey," he replied.

"Hey. Um... You got a minute," she asked.

"Yeah. What's wrong. Why you sound upset?" he asked. Alexis held the phone. She hadn't realized he knew her well enough to detect that. She thought she was doing a good job of sounding normal.

"Um. Well... I have to fly back. I've been here too long. I um...I'm going to go home today," she replied. Rome came up off the freeway and turned around headed back to his house. He wasn't sure what was wrong and why she wanted to abruptly leave. She hadn't mentioned anything when they ate breakfast together although she did seem quiet. "I'm on my way back," he said.

"What! No. No. Don't come back. I already have uber coming to get me," she said. "I'm not coming there to take you back. I'm coming to talk to you face to face," he said hanging up on her. Alexis looked at her phone for a few seconds before sitting it down. *Oh no. He's coming back!* she said. Rome called Erin and told her to postpone his meeting until the next day then called Tanasha and told her the same thing and flew home.

Rome had an uneasy feeling as he pulled up to his house. He went in quickly calling Alexis' name but the house was silent. He ran through the house and into the room she was staying in. *Damn. She left!* He said as he ran to the front door. Rome ran out the house, jumped in his car and headed for the airport. He didn't know what terminal she would possibly be at but he was going anyway. He grabbed his phone and made a call. He needed to vent and he wanted answers.

"Hello," Paula said, as she answered her ex-husbands call.

"What did you do! What did you say to her?" he yelled.

"Rome calm down. What are you talking about," she replied.

"She left. Just up and left. Why? Did you say something to make her leave? She was fine this morning," he complained.

"I talked to her and she said she wanted to go back. She said she felt conflicted about wanting you and she said she needed to go. She's in love with you. But you haven't said anything to her to let her know you feel the same. The fact that you're calling me yelling at me tells me you do. I haven't heard you yell at anyone in years. I'll call her. But I can't make her come back Rome," she said. Rome hung up and continued his drive to the JFK airport.

Paula hung up and turned to Amy. "He is really in love with her. I knew he would like her but he is completely gone over her. I have never, in the years I've known him, seen him so upset." Amy smiled. "Good. Now you can stop worrying about Romy. They can be together and she'll love him like her own." Paula grabbed her phone. She paused and reflected on everything. Her plan would foil if her sister left. Rome would be unhappy and her son wouldn't have the love of her sister to get him through her absence.

Paula thought of what to say. How to convince Alexis to forget that Rome is her brother in law and look at him in a romantic way. Paula smiled. She believed she could get Alexis to follow her heart. She believed her sister had deep feelings. Rome did not get that way on his own. He wasn't so easily won. If he was in love then Alexis probably was as well. It took two to play.

Paula called Alexis' phone. Amy watched nervously hoping her lover could work it out. Paula looked at her then shook her head. "She didn't pick up," she said. She tried several times over the next hour with no luck. "I know what. I'll get Penny involved. Damn! I gotta deal with her. She's going to give me straight attitude," Paula said, as she searched her phone. She realized she had Penny's old number then called her mother.

"Hi mom. Give me Penny's number," she said. "Paula baby. Where have you been. You never call. Why won't you call me more? Are you ok honey," she stressed, as she sounded emotional and desperate to be in her daughter's life. "I know mom. I will. I just had things to do. I wasn't in a good place. But I need to call Penny first. I'll call you back after I get off the phone with her," she stated. Priscilla gave Paula the number and Paula hung up to call Penny.

"Ohhh baby yes," Penny moaned, as she took a bite of melon while Camron smeared strawberries on her vagina so he could lick it off. Camron licked and sucked the strawberries and began fucking her pussy with his tongue. The two were in one of their kinky moods when Penny's phone rang. "Who is this now?" she said, looking at her phone. Penny jumped up and took the call. "Babe. Seriously. Who is that? You tell them I was just about to eat that pussy up," he said. Penny put her finger to her mouth. Camron laughed as he didn't realize she had already answered her phone.

"Hello," she answered, in a tone that sounded as though she was fucking at that moment. "Wow. Same old Penny. Getting your pussy ate all day long. Some things never change," Paula stated. "At least it's by a man. What do you want Paula? Yes. I'm busy having oral relations," she said, in a sarcastic voice.

"Penny. I don't have time. I see Alexis filled you in," she replied. "Alexis didn't have to tell me shit. I been knew you liked pussy Paula! Anyway... What is it?"

Paula sighed and continued. "Pebbles left my house upset. She must have boarded a plane and is already on her way there. Can you make sure she's ok? She won't answer my calls," Paula stated, sounding emotional which was a rare emotion for her.

"That's cause she's in love with Rome. You had to know that would happen. You know her and you knew it was a chance she would be unable to control her feelings for him. You knew this Paula! Now I have to help fix this shit. You have a lot of fucking nerve. You never cared about anything or anyone except yourself. She's not here! If she was, she would have called me by now. She must be on her flight still. I'll call you Paula ok," she said, fuming and too angry to talk to her sister.

Paula held the phone. She missed her sister she just didn't want to admit it. "Paula did you hear me. I said I'll call," she repeated. "Yes. Ok... I'm sorry Pen," she blurted. "For what?" Penny asked, her voice low, a hint of pain in it. "For everything and anything I ever did," she replied. Penny looked at her phone as if something about its structure had changed. She was speechless. "Did you hear me," Paula asked. "Yeah. I'll call you. Ok," Penny said, as she got off the phone.

She looked at Camron and looked away. "What's wrong?" he asked. "Nothing. She apologized to me. Wow," she stated. "For what?" he asked. "I don't know. Nothing. I can't even tell you what our problem was. It's been that long," she said, reflecting on their past. She held the phone and stared off for a moment. Then tried calling Alexis.

Hours went by as Penny anxiously waited for her phone to ring. She sent text and tried calling Alexis but nothing. She had run to Alexis' condo and to her office, which was closed. Penny was getting more worried by the minute as she sat there knowing that too many hours had gone by for Alexis to not be back in town. She called Paula in a panic. "Paula. She not here. She still not home," she said, sounding worried.

"Ok. Don't panic. If she not there by morning I'll fly there. Let's not panic though. Give her another couple of hours and then go to the police. This is not like her but she's also upset and she must not be ready to talk yet. Just wait." Penny wiped her tears and Camron hugged her as he had been trying to comfort her all day. She was showing signs of stress and he was trying to calm her down. Penny hung up from Paula and Camron went to get her a glass of juice. "Baby you have to eat," he said. I'm going to get you something. I'll be right back," he said, as he left out. Penny sat down and tried Alexis again and got her voice mail again which was now full.

P

enny heard a knock on her door and ran to open it. She stood there in a daze staring at the man who she immediately guessed, had to be Rome. He fit the description and he looked just liked she had pictured. Unbelievably fine. "Hi I'm Rome. You Penny," he asked. "Yes. I can't find Alexis. Have you talked to her?" she said. "No. Can I come in," he asked. "Oh. I'm sorry. Yes. Please come in," she said.

Rome and Penny sat on her couch as Penny told him what Alexis had said and how she felt. She confirmed what Paula had already told him which was, Alexis was in love with him but didn't think she should be and so she was trying to just come back home. Rome told Penny that he loved Alexis too and wasn't going to let her go without fighting for her. Penny envied Alexis. Rome was more than enough man and she saw why he was able to get not one but two of her sisters. And if Alexis didn't want him, she would probably be sister number three. "Where is her condo?" he asked. Penny told him then showed him how to get there. Alexis lived close by and she drew him an easy diagram and she put in in his phone GPS.

Rome went to Alexis' condo and waited in his rental car. He sat there for an hour talking to Penny and Paula, on and off, until he saw what he thought was her car coming down the drive. He watched as the car pulled up and the young lady got out. It was dark and he couldn't see the woman's face but he recognized her walk. He confirmed it when he saw her go to the right unit. He let her go in and shut the door. A minute later Penny called him.

"She's on her way home. She just called me," she said. "I know. I'm here now. She just went in," he replied, as he saw Penny pull up. "Oh, ok. I see you sitting over there. Let me go in and make sure she's ok first. Give me a minute." Penny got out of the car and knocked on Alexis' door. Rome watched as she walked in. He was anxious. He was desperate. He didn't know how she felt. The things Paula and Penny told him she never said. She never even showed.

Rome hoped he could convince her to come back. But he was up against a lot. She had a company. She had a mother and a sister that was there that she loved and cared about. She had an on/off relationship with a man that was crucial to her company's success. And she was an attractive, single, woman with no kids and the world at her finger tips. But Rome had everything else she needed so he would not be going home just yet. He had a kid that she loved, money, and the world was already in his hand. He loved her and wanted to be with her so he would complete her.

Penny talked to Alexis and never said Rome was in Atlanta, let alone outside in his car. She could tell Alexis was unaware as she cried and professed her love for him and how she felt guilty from day one for falling for him, even though Paula had given her blessing. Penny hugged her the two talked about everything that was on Alexis' mind. When Penny saw that Alexis had calmed, she told her she would be back. She told her she was leaving momentarily and would be right back. Penny left out and pulled Alexis' door partially closed so Rome could go in. She waved and pulled off and Rome got out of his car and made it up her walkway and into her condo, shutting the door behind him.

Alexis was in her bathroom in the shower and thought she heard something but assumed it was one of her neighbors. She let the water run down her face to soothe her and help alleviate her torment. She was already missing Rome and Romy and was feeling the sting of leaving. She wished she had stayed and waited on him to come back. She could have told him how she felt. She would have given him the chance to tell her how he felt. The shower water that ran down her face hid her tears that she shed as she tried to work through her pain.

Alexis cut off her shower and got out. She dried herself off and put lotion all over and looked at herself in the mirror. She thought she looked like a train wreck but she was still beautiful. She grabbed her gown and slid it on. It was late and she needed to get to bed. She had a long night ahead of her and an even longer day as she would have to show up to work and try to hide the fact that she was a devastated woman trying to get back to somewhere that felt normal. She hoped Delano wouldn't come for her. He no longer had a chance in hell and would feel her wrath. He was not Rome

A familiar smell made Alexis' heart skip a beat. It was the scent of a cologne she had become all too familiar with. She slowed her walk as her senses heightened. She continued to her bedroom, thinking it was all her imagination. Alexis walked in her room and stood dead in her tracks. She stood, staring at the love of her life. Rome sat on her bed staring back at her and smiling. "Were you going somewhere Alexis," he said, as he sat there looking intensely at her. She stood there unable to move. How was he in her condo? How did he get in Atlanta? The last time she talked to him, was back in New York.

"Why are you here? Why are you running from me? From us? I love you. I'm not letting you stay here unless I move my company here and stay here with you. Is that what you need me to do?" he asked as he stood and approached her slowly, never taking his eyes off of her. He looked her deep in her eyes. He looked like a man willing to risk everything. Alexis took a breath. It felt as though she had stopped breathing. She was speechless. Still broken. She loved him. She wanted him. But fear controlled her. The fear of the unknown.

Tears rolled down her eyes as she struggled to say anything to him, for fear it wouldn't come out right. "You don't have anything to say? Don't you know that I need you like I need air to breathe. That I'll put everything on hold to get you back. That you're my angel."

He stopped within an inch of her face. He moved in slowly and began to kiss her. He pulled her close. Alexis opened her mouth. She wanted him more than she ever wanted anything. She was happy he was there. Happy he came to get her. Her tears were tears of joy. She embraced him. He kissed her passionately, taking his time, as if he never wanted it to end. Alexis opened her gown and allowed it to fall to the floor.

"I love you and no I don't want you to move here. I'll go back with you," she said, as he wiped her tears. Rome grabbed her face and kissed her, as she guided him backwards to her bed. She pushed him down and crawled on top of him. She straddled him, as he rubbed her body gently. "I love you," he whispered in her ear. He rolled her off of him and got on top of her. Alexis moaned, as he planted soft warm kisses all over her neck and chest. They kissed passionately as they professed their love for each other.

Rome kissed her all over her face and neck slowly, taking in her smell and the moist softness of her skin. His body ached for her. He had waited on this moment. He placed tender kisses on her neck taking his time to suck her in small spots. The warmth of his mouth had Alexis burning with desire for him. She could feel him between her legs. His hard manhood felt like a thick log between the folds of her pussy. It was unbearable. She wanted him inside her but she would wait. His kisses felt good. His mouth felt wonderful. Steam came from him and his heat was good.

"Uhh," Alexis moaned as he continued driving her insane, passionately sucking on her lips then kissing her on her nose and her eye and he then made his way down to her neck. She could feel his dick pulsating and when she tried to place him inside her he pulled her hand. "No! not yet," he said, kissing her and staring into her eyes. He wiped a tear from her then kissed her once more. He took his time kissing her softly as Alexis moaned. He was methodical with the placement of each kiss sending her into a zone as she moaned and rubbed his head. "Oh, Rome baby...I need you..." she said, moaning and calling his name.

Rome worked his way down to her breast sucking her gently then moved down to her stomach. He continued down, stopping at her vagina, kissing her softly and then dove in like he was going for a gold medal. He sucked and kissed her so completely and accurately that she stopped moaning and looked down at him. She could not believe how good he was and she needed to see his face.

But he knew. Rome was a king in the bedroom and he had waited a long time to be this passionate with a woman. When he loved a woman, this was what she got. Everything times ten. Rome sucked her pussy for fifteen to twenty fabulous, unforgettable minutes than came up and entered her. Alexis had already come twice and was in tears and ready for a break which he wasn't ready to give. He needed her to remember this night. He wanted her to never forget it. Ever!

Chapter Ten – Perfection

T

he next morning Alexis woke and stared at Rome as he slept. She kissed him lightly so he wouldn't wake then continued watching him as he slept. She was deep in love and she wondered how she would ever be able to live without him. *I love this man right here!* she thought, she smiling as she grabbed her phone and slowly and quietly left the room.

Rome was in a deep and hard sleep from sheer exhaustion. He had made love to Alexis many times through the night and had only been asleep a few hours. Alexis made her way into the kitchen, still smiling and feeling completely fulfilled. She decided to call Penny to tell her about her wonderful night. She had suspected that Penny was already aware. There was no way Rome could have gotten into her condo any other way than by Penny letting him in.

"You calling me early as hell Alexis. You better be calling me to tell me you fucked that fine ass muthafucking man of yours. Please say you fucked him cause if not, I'm hanging up," Penny said. Alexis laughed. "Yes. You are so fucking stupid. Yes. I did. And yes, it was wonderful. Mind blowing. I love him. And if I say more, I'll have to kill you," she joked. Penny sat up and looked at Camron. She eased out of bed so she wouldn't wake him. He turned over and let out a light moan. Penny eased out of her room and closed her door.

"What! Yes. Oh! I'm so proud of you. He's fine too Alexis. Damn. When he knocked on my door, I thought a prayer had been answered," she said with a light chuckle. The two talked on the phone for a half hour sharing stories and Alexis constantly peeked down the hall to make sure he wasn't awaking. She didn't want any more mishaps like what had happened with Delano.

"Damn Pen. I'm so gone over him. It's that kind of love that scares you because you know you'll be devastated if something happened. I've never been in love like this before. This is scary," she confessed. "It's not really all that scary. I mean. I've been in love a few times. I'm in love now with Camron. I can't even imagine seeing anyone else. It's really a wonderful thing, not a scary thing," she replied.

"Yeah. I guess. He wants me to fly back with him in a few days. I have to try and take care of whatever business I can in a short time. I may need your help. You not working now. Can't you start working at Alexis Allen Designs?" she asked. "But I know nothing about it. What would I do?" Penny asked. "It's not complicated. I will teach you. Delano can show you too. There's a lot of money in it. And you're great with people," Alexis assured.

Penny never gave it much thought. She always made her own way as did Alexis. But it sounded like a good idea if she could get up to speed on it and then learn as she went along. "I would have to learn that business. I catch on fast but I would need Sara and Delano to help me. I can try Alexis. That's all I can do is see how it works out," she replied.

Rome awoke to the smell of turkey bacon, eggs and toast cooking. Alexis peeked in her room and saw him texting and jumped on the bed and kissed him. "Hi babe," Rome said, smiling at her. "Hey. I'm making breakfast," she said. "I see. It smells good in here," he replied, sitting his phone down and kissing on her neck.

"I have a lot to do today. I'm running to my office. Then I have to drop by my client's office and then my mom's house," she stated trying to see what he wanted to do. She had hoped he would stay behind and not want to go along, especially to her office. She did not want Delano giving him any evils eyes but luck was not on her side this morning. "I'm going with you," he replied. "I want to see your office," he stated.

"Ok. Let's leave in an hour," she said kissing him, which turned him on again and he rolled on top of her.

Rome got in the shower while Alexis talked to Sara and one of her other salesmen in the office named Patrick. She was dressed in a lavender Nicole Miller dress and Manolo pumps waiting on Rome and going through her mail. She smiled at how long he was taking in the shower. She had never seen a man shower so long and she thought it was so endearing that she sent Penny a text about it. Rome got dressed and walked into the kitchen, right up behind Alexis and kissed her on the back of her neck.

"You ready," he said, kissing her neck slowly. "Yes. We'll never get out of here if you don't stop," she replied. Rome laughed and the two headed out the door. Alexis handed him the keys to her Audi SUV so she could look over AutoCAD drawings while he drove. "I'm going to need to go to the store. I have no spare clothes," he said. "I can keep washing your stuff every morning," she replied. "No. I'll just grab something," he replied.

Rome pulled up to Alexis' office and parked in the private lot. "This is nice baby," he said. Alexis spent most of her savings making it nice. Upgrades to the sign and a new paint job helped tremendously. She even invested in several huge flower pots and statues to make the place look regal. "Thank you, baby. I just need to meet with one of my salesmen. His name is Patrick and he landed a big account while I was gone. He's been nervous about me not being here. He thinks I'm closing the business, but I'm going to try to run it from New York with Penny's assistance," she said. "She's done this type of work before?" he asked. "No. But she wants to try," she replied.

Rome didn't think it was a good idea. He was an expert in running companies and he knew that allowing someone with no experience to head a company was a bad idea. "Baby. I know she's your sister but don't you have someone more qualified to actually run it until she learns this field," he asked. "Yes and no. I mean. Patrick maybe. Delano wants to but..." she replied. "Your ex? No. He can't run it. As a matter of fact, you should fire him," he said, shaking his head. Alexis smiled. Rome was jealous and she heard it all in his voice. "No. Don't be like that. Besides. He's gonna quit anyway when he sees you," she replied. "Good."

Alexis walked in with Rome right behind her. She introduced him to her receptionist and the other staff that slowly came out to say hi to her. Alexis had seven employees that consisted of salespeople, one sales assistant and one receptionist. Delano stayed in his office, fuming and refusing to come out and speak. Rome stood around talking to the salespeople who were impressed with his credentials. He told them about his companies and how he built them up to be the powerhouses that they were through sales, marketing and determination.

Alexis walked away, smiling as she walked back to her office. She walked by Delano's office and stopped. She slowly walked in but he refused to acknowledge her presence. "Hey Delano," she said, with a meek and low tone in her voice. She knew his heart had been ripped apart and she felt bad for him. He stopped typing and looked up at her.

"You move fast. You've been gone for a few weeks and got yourself a new man already. Damn you Alexis. Look, I'm busy," he said, as he resumed typing. "I was going to tell you. I just didn't know how to say it. I know this hurts you," she said. "No, it doesn't. And when he breaks your heart, don't come looking for me to soothe it," he said.

"You're being ridiculous right now. I'm going to go to my office," she said, turning and walking out. She went to her office which was at the end of the hall facing a park. Alexis was glad to be there. She got sentimental when she sat down. She wondered if she was moving too fast. She would be going to another city and leaving behind years of cold calls, intense marketing and sleepless nights worth of work. But she loved Rome and she was not letting him leave Atlanta without her.

Sara came in and brought Alexis coffee and the rest of the drafts she was looking for. "Here's the rest of it," she said, sitting the pile down. "Thanks Sara. What's Rome doing?" she asked. "Oh. He's in with Delano," she replied. Alexis' eyes got big but she immediately pulled herself together. She didn't want to cause alarm with Sara but she would need to know, immediately, what they were talking about.

"Oh... Ok. Um thanks," she replied, as Sara walked out. Alexis jumped up and hurried towards Delano's office stopping a few feet away and standing near the door, so she could hear what the conversation was about. She instantly recognized Patrick's voice too and listened as the men talked sports, money and sales.

Alexis smiled and walked back to her office. She knew Delano was not violent but she knew nothing about what Rome was capable of given the situation. He showed innocent signs of jealousy but nothing more. She assumed he wasn't violent or confrontational but she was still getting to know him and nothing a man did surprised her. But Rome was being a complete gentleman and she was proud of him. The men were laughing and talked as if they'd known one another. It was shocking. Delano was actually laughing. The men sounded upbeat. She could relax. There was nothing to worry about.

Alexis wrapped up her work and gave Patrick clear instructions on how to proceed. She and Rome left, headed to Dalton Industries to drop off revised AutoCAD drawings and get the CEO's approval. Alexis wanted to know all the details of his talks while he was in Delano's office. "Babe. So, you talked to him," she asked, looking at him with a curious look on her face. "Yeah. I wanted to meet him. I know he wants you still. I needed him to see me and know what he was up against. It's a man thing," he said.

Alexis shook her head and looked out the window. "When we leaving?" she asked, feeling relaxed and happy to be spending time with him. "I got us tickets for Friday," he replied, reaching over to hold Alexis' hand while he drove. Alexis took his hand and smiled as he rubbed her fingers. His touch was making her want to make a beeline for her condo and jump on him naked. But Alexis realized what he'd just said and worried about the timeframe. "That's two days away," she said. "I know. Do what you need to do so we can go baby," he said. Alexis sighed and started thinking about what all she needed to do and how fast she could get it done.

Rome and Alexis pulled up to her condo at ten o'clock at night, after a long day of running around. They walked in with groceries and carry out food and relaxed. Alexis took off her clothes and ran a shower. She could hear Rome checking in on Romy and she heard him talk to the toddler and tell him that he loved him and that the two of them was coming back soon. Alexis smiled. She was ready to go back. She missed Romy. She had become quite attached to the toddler that kept her on her toes. Her phone started buzzing with a text from Penny checking up on her and Rome.

You and yo future baby daddy still good, she texted sending a smiley face along with it.

Alexis replied; *Yes. Getting ready to shower, make love, shower and make love again. Can't get enough of him.* TTYL.

The texts put a smile on her face. She was completely consumed with her feelings for him. It was great having him there in Atlanta with her. She blushed at thoughts of him. She pictured him rushing through an airport and jumping on a plane to claim his love and whisk her off to his castle. Alexis was a romantic and love the thought of Rome coming after her. After a few minutes she heard Rome come in the bathroom and he got in the shower behind her. Alexis turned to face him and walked up to him and started kissing him. Their long day of running around hadn't wore her out to the point of not wanting him. She needed him. They had a lot of fucking to do to make up for lost time.

Rome caressed her face and gazed into her eyes as he planted kisses on and around her mouth. He dove his tongue into her mouth and the kissed lovingly and rubbed her body. Alexis got out and asked him to hurry up. Rome took the quickest shower he had ever taken in his life. When he emerged, he almost lost it at the site of Alexis spread out on the bed in an enticing pose ready for him. Rome removed his towel and bypassed all her body parts going straight to her pussy and locking his arms around her so she wouldn't move.

Alexis moaned loudly as he dove into her pussy with his tongue for a full twenty minutes taking just two breaks to say erotic, freaky things before going back at it. He made circles with his tongue and suck her driving her absolutely insane with ecstasy. Alexis fucked his face like she was riding his dick, moaning so loudly that her neighbors could hear. She calmed down enough when she felt a wave of sensations and then she screamed his name as she came.

It was Friday morning and Penny was at Alexis Allen Designs, ready for her first official day of employment. She was going to start off as a sales assistant and learn the business. She walked through the doors dressed in a deep V neck blouse and work slacks tight enough to be stretch pants. Sara couldn't believe her eyes but tried to keep a straight face and not looked surprised or embarrassed at her choice of clothing.

Patrick couldn't be happier and immediately volunteered to show her around and take her under his wing. Delano, who was still acting in a more managerial role as requested by Alexis, took on the role of mentor and Penny was scheduled to make a few runs with him. "Hey Penny," he said, walking up to her. "Delano," she replied. "Let me show you to your office. It's a shared office and you'll be in there with Marty. She one of our newer salespeople," he stated.

Penny followed Delano down to the office, speaking to everyone she passed. She could already see the looks on some of the women's faces and she sighed. *What are they staring at?* she thought. Delano showed her to her office and she walked in and spoke to Marty. Marty seemed cool and Penny was glad she would be sharing a office with someone that seemed nice. Marty was a petite brunette, 5'1, and had a lot of personality. She almost talked Penny's ears off about her family, her kids and her accomplishments. Penny smiled at Delano and he left out so the two could get better acquainted. He turned back and told Penny they had their first meeting in an hour then went to his office.

"We should be leaving," Delano said. It was time for he and Penny to go to their first appointment together. Delano had a meeting with a prospective client. A company called *Viper Industries,* and it was one of his biggest deals to date. The company had many satellite offices and closing the deal could be lucrative for years to come.

As they drove, Delano poured his heart out to Penny telling her he had met Rome and although Rome seemed like a cool guy, he didn't expect them to last. Penny tried to avoid talks of Alexis and Rome's personal business and tried changing the subject but he went on nonstop about them. "Delano. Let's not talk about that. She's happy. You should be happy for her even though you aren't with her now. You started out as friends first. She cares about you. Let her be happy. You know she deserves it," she said, watching the landscape as he drove down the highway. "I do want her to be happy. I just don't understand why she couldn't be happy with me."

Penny listen to Delano express himself over the love he lost. She tried to be a comfort to him. She felt sorry for him. Alexis wasn't coming back. Their love affair was over. And she hoped he could tuck his wounded heart inside his chest and move on.

She checked her phone expecting to get a text from Alexis when she touched down. This was the day her and Rome would be flying back to New York and Penny wanted to hear from her so she would know they made it back safe. Penny hated flying and wouldn't be total at ease until Alexis was back home. Penny and Delano pulled up to Viper and walked up to the huge building with mirrored windows. She became instantly tense and she hoped she would impress the client and make a good impression.

It was important to Penny to do well. Her sister needed her to succeed at this as they had talked of Penny running the company one day especially with Delano jealousy which made him unpredictable. "You'll be ok," Delano assured, noticing her nervousness. After an hour with the decision makers of the company, Penny and Delano emerged smiling. He was impressed with Penny's ability to talk to people and sell the company. She had no real experience and he was shocked how knowledgeable she appeared. It was obvious she had been doing some up-front research. "You did good. I think we got his one," he said. "Thanks."

R

ome and Alexis arrived in New York and got in Rome's Suburban and headed home. Alexis had tried to talk him into letting her stay an additional day before they flew back home but Rome was against it. She didn't understand his hesitation but suspected it had something to do with Delano. He again, tried to talk her into letting him go but she told him to give her time. She tried explaining to him that she couldn't do such a thing so soon and that he was harmless, but Rome new better. Delano's behavior told a different story. He was a man in love and Rome was not taking any chances.

"Romy. Hi baby," she exclaimed as the toddler ran to her and Rome from the porch of his uncle Nigel's house. Nigel was Rome's older brother and he had met Alexis once before. Alexis liked him. He seemed supportive of them and she appreciated how welcoming he and his wife Karen were. She thought he was just as handsome and down to earth as Rome was. She liked the way they were with the women and children in their lives. "Hey," he said, greeting them in his driveway. Rome picked Romy up and put him in his car seat and then talked to his brother for a minute while Alexis sat in the back seat with the toddler. She played with him and gave him a snack as they waited on Rome. After several minutes, he walked back to the car and they headed home.

Chapter Eleven – The Other Misses

R

ome and Alexis adjusted to their new lives, happily committed to each other and focused on their future. Alexis was flying back and forth to Alexis Allen Designs every two weeks to keep it going and to help Penny get acclimated. Rome hated her trips there and would anxiously count the days until she came back. He was still pressuring her to fire Delano but she couldn't because it was Delano's hard work and knowledge that was keeping the company growing. Alexis flew back like clockwork, every other Friday and would stay until Monday evening.

Life was hectic, but no matter how busy she got both her and Rome made plenty of time for each other. She had started looking into working with New York companies. She was back, knocking on doors and introducing herself to the smaller businesses there. She was slowly getting her company off the ground with Rome's help but New York was saturated with design firms and she found it hard to come in on a markets heavily flooded field with many powerful firms that had strong connections and could offer the clients deeper discounts and a wider selection. But Alexis took her time. She didn't need the money. Her company back home was still thriving and Rome had plenty of money. She relaxed with the pressure off and took her time with Alexis Allen Designs New York.

Alexis worked long hours cold calling but seemed to be making no headway. She thought of giving up. Rome was committed to her succeeding and had decided to take on a more vital role and let her work with some of his loyal happy clients. He could see she was losing her zest and feared losing her to the draw of her business in Atlanta. But he was wrong in his fears. Alexis was in New York because of him and would be there with him unless he said otherwise. What he would need to realize is that she loved him more than she loved Alexis Allen Designs.

"Hey baby. What you doing?" Rome asked, missing her and checking in with her. It was Saturday and he had two more days before she would be back home. They had been together six months now and he had a surprise for her. "Hi. I'm missing you that's what I'm doing," she replied, smiling and going through papers. "Penny and I are going through an AutoCAD drawing and an order. I'm showing her how to double check the designers work. What you doing?" she asked. "Waiting on Monday," he replied.

Alexis smiled. She missed him every time she left and she knew the feeling was mutual. She counted the days until she could travel less, but Penny still had a lot more to learn an understand, even though she had made significant strides. Penny smiled and walked out to go get a cup of coffee and give her sister privacy.

"I wish you didn't have to keep going there," he commented. "I know. I wish I didn't either. But she's almost where I need her to be. She's smart. It's only been six months and she's doing great. She has good business sense. She catches on quick and she knows how to land the accounts. I had to tell her to tone down her wardrobe though. Some of my employees thought she was turning off women executives with the way she dresses," she replied. "But things are better now," she added, as she looked over her new client contracts.

Rome paced his floor. He had things he was worried about but didn't want to change the mood of the conversation. But it drove him crazy not saying anything to her so he did. "Have you seen Delano?" he asked. Alexis held the phone. She wished he wasn't so preoccupied with him. He was not an issue for her and she wasn't going to let him be. Delano was staying in his lane and not bothering her for the moment and she still was not ready to let him go. She would feel terrible letting him go just because of Rome's jealousy. But she understood why, she just didn't have the heart to do it and now, Penny needed him. Penny wouldn't make it in the business without him.

"No. He had a lot of appointments today. And he doesn't work on weekends so I won't be seeing him. Why are you still worried about him?" she asked. "Don't ask me that Alexis. You know why. He's your ex. This is not good. He still wants you," Rome said, with a tense voice.

"Rome please. Just give me time. Nothing's happening. You know I wouldn't do that. He's showing Penny the ropes. She needs him," she replied. "No. You need him," he replied, sounding upset. Alexis felt helpless at that point. She was not ready to let Delano go and she couldn't even picture herself doing so. He had landed major accounts for the company. She had never fired anyone. Delano hired and fired the employees. And he hadn't done anything. He was being cordial. Alexis knew he probably still loved her but he was staying in his lane.

Alexis spoke with Rome for several more minutes before getting off the phone and going to find Penny. Penny was standing in the lobby talking to Camron who had stopped by to see what the women were up to. "Hey Cam," Alexis said, in a melancholy voice. Penny looked at her then kissed Camron. "I'll see you later babe. We still have some things to finish," she said. Camron said his goodbyes and left. "Ok. What's wrong?" she said. "Nothing. Rome's pressing me to fire Delano," she said. "What. Alexis no. He hasn't done anything," she replied. "I know. Try telling him that. I think I'm going to go home early. He sounded more upset this time. He's growing tired of the trips. He's letting his imagination run off with thoughts of me and Delano when nothing is happening. Delano hasn't even flirted with me. It's strictly business now," she said. "I'll go home and surprise him," she said, smiling and hopeful that she could get him back in a good mood and get his mind off of Delano.

Alexis rose on Sunday morning ready to get to the airport and head back home. She got out of bed feeling a little tired and wanted to lay back down. She felt as though she was coming down with something but she was not going to let anything stop her from going back home. She rolled her bag to her waiting cab and left her condo. She had stopped driving her car back and forth to the airport deciding to leave it at the condo instead. She reached the Hartsfield-Jackson Airport and walked through headed to Concourse C. When she got on the plane, she settled in for her flight and pulled out her favorite magazine and flipped through the pages. She always flew first class but no matter the accommodations, Alexis hated the excessive travel. First class or not, something had to give.

Camron and Penny were stretched out, legs entangled watching tv. Camron was eating popcorn and occasionally feeding them to Penny. "Open up bae," he said, as he popped a kernel in her mouth. Penny smiled. She looked over when her phone caught her eye. It had lit up signifying a text or call. She picked it up and noticed a missed call from Paula. She hadn't heard from her in a few months. The two had talked on and off and were trying to get past their issues and reconcile. Penny looked perplexed. She wouldn't have expected to hear from her so soon. "This is Paula baby. I'm going to call her back in the other room," she said. Camron shook his head and continued to watch the game. It was Sunday and he planned on watching games all day with his woman.

"Hello," she answered. "Hey Paula. It's Penny. What's up," she said. "Penny," she said, in a voice she almost didn't recognize. "Yeah. What's going on," she replied. "Everything... I'm at my house. I'm here with Romy. Our housekeeper Ann told me Alexis was there with you. She's not picking up. I needed to talk to her," she replied. "What do you mean your house. The house in New York that Alexis now lives at with Rome?" she asked, worried about what Paula was getting ready to say. Penny braced herself for the answer. "Yes. I want to come back home," she said. "What Paula! Are you fucking insane. I will fucking kill you. If you hurt her like that, I will hunt you down and fucking kill you. Where's Rome. Put him on this muthafucking phone right now," she yelled.

Camron jumped up and walked into the front room. Penny was inconsolable and full of rage. "Rome's not here. Stop yelling. Don't you think I feel bad about all of this," she replied. "No bitch. I don't think you do. You just want what you want when you want it and you don't give a fuck who you hurt in the meantime. She's on her way there now and so am I," she said, hanging up on Paula. Camron tried to hug her but she pushed him away. "I have to get a flight to New York now," she said. "Penny. Alexis can handle herself. You don't need to go there," he said. "Yes I do," she said, as tears rolled down her face. "That bitch," she replied.

Rome was at Nigel's house watching the game with his other brother Barron and completely unaware that Paula had arrived in town, unannounced and was at his home. Nigel was the oldest and had a wife and kids. He was a lawyer who worked closely with Rome on things that required his services. He was a handsome thirty seven year old, with a nice build on his tall 6'1 frame. He loved his brothers and threw a lot of parties and cookouts in order to keep their families close.

He and Rome were the closest and spoke frequently on the phone. They were heavily involved in each other's lives, making play dates for their children often. The two traveled together with their families and told each other their darkest secrets. Barron was the youngest and worked as a pharmacist. He was gorgeous and a bit of a player. He was thirty one years old and was the youngest Wade sibling. Brother's Tyrus and Donovan were both busy and couldn't make the game day, that Nigel always held on Sundays. The brothers all looked a lot alike and were all accomplished men.

Rome laughed, yelled and enjoyed the game as his phone sat on the table next to him. He was unaware of the calls Paula had made as he cheered his team on. She wanted to locate him and talk to him before Alexis got back but she didn't realize that Rome didn't have her new number and wouldn't have answered it.

"Rome. What's up with Paula. Did you two come to an agreement about Romy?" Barron asked.

Nigel looked at his brother to see if he had anything more to say about the situation. Rome had already told him what was going on as the two talked frequently but Barron was only partially aware of the issues. He knew that Paula had left for London and had stayed and had just been made aware of who Alexis was.

"No. She won't agree to giving me sole custody. She's procrastinating on signing anything. I may have to take her to court. All I know is she not getting him," he said.

Alexis got off the plane and caught a cab home, trying to relax but was anxious to see Rome. She knew he would be happy to see her since she was a whole day early and she needed to see him. She wanted to show him that he was the most important person in her life. She wanted to tell him that she'd canceled other travel dates and wasn't planning to go back to Atlanta for two months. As she pulled up in her driveway, she saw the front door open. She smiled as she assumed Rome saw the cab drive up the lengthy driveway and had opened it for her. She got out and paid the driver and rolled her bag up to the door, wondering why he wasn't standing in it. Something didn't seem right. Then she thought maybe Ann had opened the door.

Alexis walked in and stopped. She stood there frozen and in shock. "Pebbles," Paula said, walking up to her and hugging her. Alexis did not hug her back. She was afraid to move. What was Paula doing there. If she was returning, why hadn't she called to say so. And where was Rome. "What are you doing here Paula?" she said, looking worried and still unable to move.

"Um. Well. I know that this is going to sound crazy and I don't want you to get mad at me. Please Pebbles. Please don't hate me but..." she said, pausing and trying to give Alexis a moment.

"I want to come back home. I miss my family. I just can't do it anymore. I'm sorry. I didn't realize this would be such a struggle," she confessed. A tear rolled down Alexis' cheek. She shook her head, remaining silent and never taking her eyes off of her sister.

"Say something Pebbles. Please. I'm sorry. I'll give you money. Anything. Just don't hate me," she said.

Alexis stared at her then walked into the kitchen, grabbed the first set of keys she saw and walked to the garage. She was completely distraught as she hit the button, prepared to drive whichever car opened when she hit it. Rome's black Ferrari alarm sounded and she hit it again, unlocking the doors and then looked around for the garage door opener. The garage was a five-car attached garage and she couldn't find the remote to open the door so she opened it manually, got in the car and pulled off. Paula stood on the porch, tears rolling down her face and watched as Alexis took off down the street.

Alexis cried hysterically as she drove 90 mph down the expressway headed back to the airport. *I knew it. I knew something like this would happen,* she said, as she continued driving. Within minutes Alexis was being followed by a cop who was gaining on her. His lights came on but Alexis continued to drive. After a minute she pulled over and wiped her eyes. The cop held his hand on his gun as he approached the black Ferrari with tinted windows. He knocked on the window and Alexis rolled it down.

"Ok mam. You want to step out of the vehicle, he said. Alexis got out and refused to look at him. The cop instantly saw she had been crying and calmed down, taking his hand off his gun.

"Did you realize you were going 100 miles per hour mam," he asked.

"No," she replied, wiping her eyes and looking away from him.

"What's going on mam?" he asked.

Alexis burst out crying telling the cop that her sister wanted her husband back and that she was in love with him and she knew it was too good to be true. Alexis went on and on. The cop felt so bad for her that he told her he wasn't going to give her a ticket and that it was not a good idea to drive while so emotional because accidents happen when you're not paying attention.

Alexis apologized as she wiped her eyes. The cop stared at Alexis then got back in his car. Alexis got in the Ferrari and sat on the side of the road as the cop pulled slowly along the side of her.

"Don't sit here too long. People swerve and I wouldn't want you to get side swiped. I know you need to get yourself together, just be careful," he said, smiling at her.

"I won't. I just need a minute," she replied. The cop pulled off and Alexis sat there still in disbelief and trying to figure out if she should go back to Atlanta.

Chapter Twelve – An Unstoppable Love

R

ome was enjoying his brother's company and the three talked as they watched their game. Rome picked up his phone and saw missed calls from Penny and an unknown number. He called Penny back. "Hello," she answered, sounding upset. "Penny this Rome. What's going on? I saw you called," he said, worried something was going on with Alexis.

"Rome. Have you talked to Alexis or Paula? Where are you? Are you home?" she said, still sounding stressed.

"Not since yesterday night. She hasn't call me yet. And why would I talk to Paula. What's going on?" he said, now in full alert mode.

"Paula is there. She's at the house. Alexis is on her way there. She wanted to surprise you and come home early but Paula is at your house. She will be devastated. Paula said she wants to come back home with you," she said.

"What!" Rome jumped up and without saying another word, waved bye at his brother's and walked out the door still talking to Penny. Nigel ran out behind him,

"What's up Rome?" he asked.

"I gotta go. I'll call you in a minute," he replied.

Rome flew home, doing 100 mph hour and spotted a Ferrari off to the side of the road on the opposite side of the freeway that looked a lot like his. He thought for a minute but then shook off any thoughts that it was. Alexis didn't care for that car and Paula wouldn't dare. He pulled up to his house and saw his garage door opened and his Ferrari gone. Worry now turned to fear as he ran to the door and hurried inside. That Ferrari was a twenty minute drive away and probably gone *was* his. As he walked through his home, he heard Paula talking. He walked straight to the kitchen and stood there in shock.

"Rome," she said, smiling at him. He stood there. He looked at Ann. "Ann. Please give me and Paula a moment. Can you take Romy to the park," he said, never taking his eyes off of Paula. Paula was nervous. She had never seen him this way. He was dry, serious and his look was unyielding.

"Rome I..." she said, before being cut off by him. "Don't you say a word to me. You wait until my confused son is out of here, then we'll talk," he said.

Paula swallowed hard. She thought that he would be glad to see her. She underestimated his feelings for Alexis and she now knew, she had made a terrible mistake. Rome walked with Ann and Romy to the door, carrying the toddler and sitting him down on his toy car. He kissed Romy and spoke with Ann as Paula watched, unable to hear what he was saying.

Rome watched them for a few minutes, as they walked down the driveway, then turned to the house and came inside. Paula backed away from the door.

"Rome just listen to me for a minute," she begged.

"Alright," he said, looking at her. She saw his coldness and it suddenly gave her pause. Paula looked around weighing what she would say. How she could get him back. What she could say to get past this wall he had up. The resentment he had. The betrayal he felt.

"I want to come back home. I made a mistake. I'm not happy there. I'm not happy with her. I thought I would be, but I realize that I love you and I want us to try again. I know you love Alexis but we have a family," she pleaded, walking up to him hoping to persuade him.

"Where's my Ferrari? Is that her? Did you tell her this?" he said, with enough ice to freeze a lake.

"Um…Yeah…She came here and then she left," she said. Rome put his hands over his face is disbelief. He rubbed his eyes and then told Paula exactly how he felt.

"You can't come here. You're not welcome. You'll never be welcome. She lives here. I love her more than I am even capable of loving you. The only person here who loves you is Romy and we will go to court over him if you try to take him. The whole world knows you abandoned him. You won't get him. You don't even want him… Have you realized that you fuck up, everything you touch. You fucked your family up and abandoned them. It took years for them to recover. You tried to fuck me up, but I'm too strong. And you're trying to fuck my son up and I'm not going to let you. What happened in London? You fucked her up too probably. You need to leave and do not try and contact Pebbles cause now she's fucked up. That's my wife. She just doesn't know it yet. So you don't have a chance in hell of coming back here."

Paula stood there in total shock. She had never heard Rome talk that way. She had never seen him so serious but she saw he meant every word. Rome walked to the door and opened it and Paula left out. She cried as she walked to her car and pulled off. Rome jumped in his car hoping that his Ferrari was still on the side of the road.

Rome sighed when he saw the car gone. He called Ann and told her that Nigel was coming to get Romy and that he needed to be alone. Rome was distraught over Alexis being missing and needed to be home to plan his next move and he wanted no distractions. He called Alexis' phone repeatedly but she never answered. He called Penny and she had no answers and had been waiting on him for an update. Alexis had not answered her calls either and the two worried themselves in a panic.

Rome checked flights that had left but Alexis wasn't shown to be on any of them. He then worried that she decided to drive herself home. He didn't know what to think. Rome grabbed his phone out of desperation and called his mother. The one whose advice was always sound, correct and from the heart. The woman who raised him and his four brothers to be strong, capable men. The woman who would be able to give him advice about another woman because she was one herself.

"Hello," Glady's answered, as she sat on her couch playing Sudoku and waiting for her food to get done.

"Hi ma. You busy?" he asked.

"No. I got a roast in the oven that's almost done. What's going on honey," she asked.

"I need some advice but first I have to be straight with you," he stated.

"Ok honey. Whatever it is I'm sure it will work out," she replied. Gladys supported her sons and although she meddled in their personal lives, she was always well intended and she was usually right.

"I've been seeing someone. Her name is Alexis and she is Paula's younger sister," he said, pausing to see her reaction before proceeding.

"How did that happen Rome? How did you end up involved with her sister?" she asked. Rome spent an hour telling his mother the details of how everything went down. She got up to shut her oven off and sat back down, silent and shocked by how the two met and fell in love. But she could hear it in her sons' voice that he was head over heels in love with her and so she would need to help him get his head right and then find his love.

"She's close to her family so she probably went home. She's devastated and when a woman is devastated, we usually seek out those closest to us for comfort. Did you check the airlines?" she asked.

"Yes. And they don't have her on any of the flights to Atlanta." Just as Rome talked, he realized that he hadn't checked under the name Pebbles. That he searched using the name *Alexis Allen*. "Mom, I gotta call you back. I just remembered something."

Rome called the airlines back and was told that a Pebbles Allen had in fact, boarded Delta 180, bound for Atlanta GA. He booked a flight but would have to wait nearly four hours before he could leave. He called Penny to see if she heard anything.

"Hey it's Rome. Did Alexis call you?" he asked.

"No Rome. I still haven't talked to her," she replied sounding tense.

"Penny I know she's there. I don't believe you. I know you've talked to her by now. You're the first person she would have called. Please tell me," he pleaded. Penny paused then told him she had spoken with Alexis.

"Yes. I'm sorry Rome. She just can't deal right now and so I just couldn't say anything," she replied. "I'm on my way there," he stated.

"No Rome. Don't! She's not even home. She doesn't want to see you right now. If you come here you won't be able to find her. Just wait. Let things calm down. She'll call you when she's ready. The only thing she told me was to tell you that your car is in area F3 inside the structure. She said it's closest to the side near the runway," she replied. Rome got off the phone and sat on his bed completely devastated and emotional. All he could do was wait

Days turned into weeks, weeks turned into months and the months dragged out to the slowest and most devastating year for Rome Wade. Alexis never called. It was like a dream he'd had and now he was living a daily nightmare, apart from the love of his life. He woke after getting enough sleep to start his day and get his son to Nigel's house. Nigel's wife Karen was now a stay at home mom after quitting her job in insurance sales to raise her three young children.

Nigel and Karen had volunteered to help out with Romy to take some of the pressure off of Gladys. Gladys tried to be Romy's caregiver, but she just couldn't keep up with the rambunctious four year old. Rome thought it was better for him if he was over Nigel's where he could play all day long with his young cousins.

Nigel walked to his car and opened the back door and got Romy out of the car seat. He noticed Rome's somber mood immediately but chose not to ask questions that he already knew the answers to. Rome had talked to him almost daily, about Alexis to the point of tiring Nigel. He would call Nigel late at night if he needed to vent or if he was having a rough day, so Nigel needed a break. He felt caught up in this emotional rollercoaster and had hoped Alexis would at least call his brother.

"He'll be ok. You want him to spend the night with us. You probably need a break from him. Let us keep him a few days while you get a break," Nigel proposed. "Yeah. He can. I'll have to bring him extra clothes over," he replied. "No. We have stuff for him. Besides, he and Bryan are the same size. Don't worry about it," Nigel replied.

Rome went back home to an empty house and tried to take his mind off of Alexis. Some days were better than others but he thought of her often and this day was one of the worst. It seemed like everything reminded him of her. Certain songs, television programs, even the way his son now wanted to be read to nightly before bed, all reminded him of Alexis. He had convinced himself that she must have been in love with someone in Atlanta otherwise she would have called to check on him. He was shocked that she hadn't even called to check on Romy.

I have to get over her. She's never coming back, he said to himself, as he sat there. Rome got up and went over to his built-in bar and poured himself a glass scotch, something he never used to do. He wasn't really a drinker but had used it to dull his pain the last several months. Rome looked forward to the day he didn't think of her so much. He thought time would heal his wounds but he hadn't made much headway.

Rome walked in *Impact Digital* to meet with a client and take care of a backlog of issues that had been sitting in a pile. He wasn't as focused as he usually was and his employees had to work harder to do things themselves that he did with ease. He was much more knowledgeable than them and whenever they faltered, he was there to pick up the pieces. But now it was the other way around. They were picking up the pieces for him. They all thought that his change in behavior was the result of his divorce from Paula, totally unaware of what was really going on in his personal life.

It had been over a year since he seen or heard anything regarding Alexis. She hadn't reached out to him. Penny wouldn't take his calls. He avoided Paula like the plague. Only talking over the phone and only talking about Romy. But he always made sure to ask if she talked to Alexis. Even though time had passed, he was still feeling the effects of his break up as if it had just happened. Time had not healed his emotional scars. Alexis affected him in their short but time together.

Rome met with his client then walked to his office and sat there. He looked at the pile and sighed. He put his hands on his head and leaned forward on his desk. He was tired, stressed and still missing Alexis. Rome sat there for several more minutes then got up and left. As he drove his phone rang. It was Tanasha, his secretary at *Impact*. "Hey. What about the papers you were supposed to sign," she said, sounding worried.

"Have Ron sign them. I have to take a trip. I won't be back for a couple of days. Have Ron call me," he stated. Rome packed his bags and was headed for Atlanta. He wanted to see Alexis one last time. He wasn't sure what he would say and didn't understand why he felt so compelled to see her after a year but he was determined to go. He knew he couldn't go another day without seeing her one last time.

I t was a warm and beautiful day in Atlanta when Rome got off the plane and made his way through the airport. His flight was uneventful, despite the efforts of the flight attendant and a female passenger, to flirt with him. No matter what was going on in his life, he was still fine as hell and was still a main attraction with women wherever he went. Rome walked to Avis car rental and picked up his car and left, headed to Alexis' condo. When he got there, he stared at the window. The condo didn't seem right. Something was off.

Rome got out of his car and walked up to the condo and looked in. It was empty. Rome sighed and looked around. He stood there for a minute. He knew it was a long shot, going to Atlanta, to see a woman who obviously didn't want to be seen. A woman whose heart had been broken and who never reached out to him. A woman who never even reached out to her sister. The sister that was responsible for the hurt and pain she felt. Rome had talked to Paula with regards to Romy and had asked if she talked to Alexis and her answer was always the same. *No!* Rome got in his car. He remembered where Penny lived and decided to pay her a visit.

Penny was cleaning her apartment when Rome knocked at her door. "One moment," she yelled. "Rome," she said, shocked to see him.

"Hey. Can I come in?" he asked, hesitating as it was obvious, she had mixed feelings about him showing up at her door.

"Yes," she said, smiling at him but nervous. "Does Alexis know you're here," she asked.

"No. She never returned my calls. Then she changed her phone number a few months ago. I need to see her Penny. I have to see her one more time. I just have to," he said.

"I'll call her Rome. I'll talk to her. Give me the hotel you're staying at and I'll let her know. If she wants to talk, she will contact you. I don't know what else to say," she stressed, looking at him and hoping he would be returning back to New York. She didn't think Alexis would want Rome popping up on her.

Rome left Penny's apartment and considered returning to New York. He knew it was a bad idea to come looking for her but when she changed her number, she left him with few options. He knew that Penny was probably calling Alexis at that moment to warn her that he was in town. He decided to go to Alexis Allen Designs. He wasn't sure what he would do when he got there. He wasn't sure about anything but this was his last attempt so he would make it count.

Rome saw Alexis' Audi and smiled. Something about seeing her car made him feel as though he was closer to seeing her. He parked directly across from it and sat. Her office overlooked the park with a slight view of the parking lot at an angle. Rome sat there looking at her office window. He wanted to walk over and look in but decided against it. He knew she was inside and that she would eventually have to come out.

It was nearing five o'clock and she would be coming out sooner rather than later. Rome sat back, listened to music and waited. After nearly an hour, Alexis emerged with Delano walking behind her. Rome sat up and smiled but his smile turned to pain when he saw that Delano was carrying a small infant in a car seat.

He watched as Delano put the baby in the back seat, hand Alexis something and then walk back in the office. Alexis got in her car and appeared distracted and didn't look over at Rome. He sat there, torn apart and emotional, as she took a call. He could see her lips moving and then he noticed and abrupt mood change as Alexis looked around.

She finally stopped when she saw his car and just looked at him. She stared at him for several minutes. It seemed tears were rolling down her face but Rome was not close enough to tell. The stress and pain in her eyes were enough. Their locked gaze hit him hard. His love for her was never more real. She was the real Mrs. Wade.

Alexis started her car and pulled off, looking over at him as she passed him. He sat there for a minute, more devastated then when he arrived. Alexis had a baby. Her and Delano were parents.

Rome was beside himself with sorrow. She was gone. No longer his and no longer available. She seemed content. She had no looks of sadness or disconnect. She seemed connected. She appeared to have connected with Delano and living a good life. She didn't get upset until she saw him. His presence made her upset. So, he was going home. Never to return.

Rome walked into his suite at the Four Seasons and walked over to the window. He looked out at the beautiful city that was home to the only woman he would ever want to be with. He now had to figure out how he would live without her. It was obvious to him that she was over their love affair and had moved on. She moved on to the rival that was there waiting with open arms. The man he worried about and tried to get rid of. They had a child now and she would never be coming back. Her face still held pain and he saw it when she looked at him. He saw the type of pain in her face that one would expect to see after something terrible had just occurred. As if the events that ripped her apart had only recently happened. Not twelve long painful months prior. He had to return home. He would never need to return again. She was gone and there was nothing he could do about it.

Rome cut his tv on. His flight was leaving at six o'clock in the morning. He barely ate the medium cooked Filet Mignon and potatoes he ordered. The only thing missing from the meal was two bites from the steak and a few spoons of potatoes. Rome flipped through the channels and watched the news followed by a late-night talk show. He was drifting off to sleep when he heard a knock at the door. He looked over at his clock. It was one a.m. He walked to his door and looked out the peephole but the person was looking down. The hall was dimly lit and so he opened the door.

Alexis stood there with the car seat in her hand and tears in her eyes. She walked past a stunned and shocked Rome who thought he was dreaming for a moment until he smelled her perfume. It was definitely her. He would know her smell with his eyes closed.

Alexis walked over to the sofa and sat the baby next to her. Rome slowly approached. She didn't say anything to him. He watched as she took the infant, dressed in a pink onesie, out of the car seat. She laid her the couch, placing a pillow beside her, so she wouldn't roll over.

"I needed to see you Alexis. You changed your number. Refuse to ever call me. I tried to give you time to stop hating me but you never called me. Ever. How could you just erase me from your heart like that," he said, sounding sad and hurt by the months of her absence.

Alexis stood up and walked to him. She got close to him. She looked at him with eyes that held the pain of a woman whose worst fears came to life. "I never thought you were mine. I felt like I was borrowing you. Like you were on loan. I didn't understand how she could leave such a wonderful man and the fact was she hadn't. She went away, to play in the sand with her playmate, and she came back. I know Paula. When she wants something, she gets it. She would have never left you alone. She wanted you back so I left," she said, crying and wiping her face.

"And you never call me. You never ask me anything. Never allow me to show you what you mean to me. What made you think she could come back? She couldn't come back after you. Not ever. I threw her out my house. I haven't seen her since. She's seen Romy once since then. And she had to go to Nigel's to see him because I refused to look at her. She's back in London. I don't love her. I loved you. I love you more than I have ever loved her. I had a ring Alexis. I was going to ask you to marry me. And now you have a baby with him," he said, being more emotional than she ever saw him.

Alexis ran to him and kissed him intensely. He had said a lifetime of words. Enough to fill her heart for an eternity. They kissed with intense passion, moaning as if they were making love. She stopped and stared at him. A single tear rolling down her cheek. Rome wanted her back. Baby and all. No matter what the outcome. If she now had a baby daddy to deal with then that would be their new life. It was Alexis' call. He wanted her to chose him.

Rome wiped the tear. He rubbed her cheek and exhaled sharply. He was ready to talk about it. About him. The baby's father. How their lives would change and how he was ready to make things work out. Alexis stared deeply at him then looked down. She knew he was confused. He didn't know about the baby. And she was still hurt by Paula words. Up until he said the most passionate and intense words a man could ever say to a woman. She knew he loved her. And she loved him.

"Are you married to him?" he asked, holding her face and looked intensely in her eyes.

"No! I'm not even with him. He was just helping get her in the car. I didn't go back to him. I still loved you. I thought you would take Paula back, so I stayed away. I can't even talk to her. I won't. Not yet," she said. Alexis paused. Rome gave an intense gaze. The love coming from him was filling the room. Alexis' mood shifted. He was there. Her love. Her man. Fighting for her. Refusing to lose. Coming to get his girl. She stared intently at him. He had something of hers.

"Where's my ring?" she asked. Rome smiled. He had it. He would always have it until it found its way on her finger.

He pulled a small black satin bag from his pocket and took out a 3.5 Karat ring. Alexis was floored. It was the most beautiful ring she had ever seen. She cried over this moment. He was there and he had a ring. He was there to ask her to marry him. She assumed Paula would wiggle her way back and realized she'd underestimated how Rome felt about her. His love for her ran deep and he was there a year later to fight for her, again.

Alexis smiled at him and pulled him to her, kissing him, then looked at him. "There's something I have to tell you," she said pausing and looking deeply in his eyes. She could feel his love for her. It was strong. It persevered. And she had a surprise for him.

"I was pregnant when I left. But I was scared. I thought there was a chance you still loved Paula and I didn't want to come in-between that," she said, pausing then looking intensely in his eyes.

"This is your daughter. Her name is Alexandria and she's yours and were ready to come home," she said, tears forming in the corners of her eyes. Rome stood in shock then looked back at the baby.

"Mine?" he asked.

"Yes. And so am I. Now will you take me home. I want to go home."

Rome grabbed Alexis and pulled her to him. His eyes peered intensely into her. Alexis "I love you. I will always love you. I want more babies. I want you forever," he said. Alexis kissed him passionately. He had her from the moment she got off the plane. It was a complicated love, but it was love no less. Paula would need to find another life.

She couldn't apologize for what resulted. She felt no guilt because it was never her intention to fall in love with him. He was a wonderful man. She was a decent and good woman. This was their life and they had her sister to thank for it. She was sure Paula was off doing Paula. More selfish decisions designed to help her get what she wanted.

Rome walked over to the baby and took her out the car seat and kissed her on the head, and smelled her hair. Alexis smiled as she watched him bond with her. She could see how happy she had made him. She could see his instant love for his baby girl. She was mentally prepared to deal with Paula if she tried another move on the family that was now hers. Rome was going to be her husband and they had a baby.

She knew Romy needed his mother and she planned on helping Paula and Rome work out some type of parenting schedule but Paula was not getting Rome back. Alexis hoped to one day rebuild the sister love they once had after things calmed down. It would be a slow road. But she was open to it. She loved her still.

Rome walked over to her and kissed her. His bright smile showing the joy he felt inside. He'd almost lost the love of his life. The only woman in the world he wanted to spend the rest of his life with.

"You ready?" he asked.

"Yes," she replied.

"Let's go home."

If you enjoyed this book try another full length novel guaranteed to have you hungrily turning the pages to see what happens next! The first book in a series from author Smokey Moment.

[Click Here](1)

---

1. https://www.amazon.com/Rocks-Stones-Between-Rose-reverse-ebook/dp/ B07FHSSY2Z/

More Books By Smokey Moment

Standalones

The Twin[2]
Wreckless[3]
Love Lies & Dirty Agendas[4]
Everything I Want[5]
Secrets, Lies & Video[6]
Keeping Him Quiet[7]
Gifted[8]
Through The Wires[9]
Beauty is Sleeping[10]
Baby Girl[11]
His Many Wives[12]

Two-part Sagas, Series or Trilogies:

Ways of Kings I[13]

---

2. https://www.amazon.com/Twin-Smokey-Moment-ebook/dp/B07ZXMLPG4/

3. https://www.amazon.com/French-Kissed-urban-romance-fiction-ebook/dp/B07HTKYN5W/

4. https://www.amazon.com/Love-Dirty-Agendas-Smokey-Moment-ebook/dp/B089R68985/

5. https://www.amazon.com/Everything-I-Want-urban-romance-ebook/dp/B07FC5SS36/

6. https://www.amazon.com/Secrets-Lies-Video-Smokey-Moment-ebook/dp/B07QLFQGR9/

7. https://www.amazon.com/Keeping-Quiet-urban-fiction-novel-ebook/dp/B07GXCTB7M/

8. https://www.amazon.com/Gifted-urban-romance-Smokey-Moment-ebook/dp/B07G6QGMDY/

9. https://www.amazon.com/Through-Wires-Smokey-Moment-ebook/dp/B07ZXVG7KK/

10. https://www.amazon.com/Beauty-Sleeping-Smokey-Moment-ebook/dp/B07SGPH3DM/

11. https://www.amazon.com/Baby-Girl-urban-fiction-novel-ebook/dp/B07JM49H13/

12. https://www.amazon.com/His-Many-Wives-Contemporary-Romantic-ebook/dp/B084NB1X94/

<u>Ways of Kings II</u>[14]
<u>Stray I</u>[15]
<u>Stray II New Life</u>[16]
<u>Stray III Covenant</u>[17]
<u>Rocks and Stones Between a Rose Part I</u>[18]
<u>Rocks and Stones Between a Rose Part II</u>[19]
<u>Pretty Fin</u>[20]
<u>Pretty Fin II</u>[21]

---

13. https://www.amazon.com/Ways-Kings-Paranormal-Werewolf-Shifter-ebook/dp/B07V68VSBK/

14. https://www.amazon.com/Ways-Kings-Paranormal-Shifter-Romance-ebook/dp/B07WRFLQPM/

15. https://www.amazon.com/Stray-paranormal-romance-werewolf-shifter-ebook/dp/B07HCQJB31/

16. https://www.amazon.com/Stray-New-Life-paranormal-werewolf-ebook/dp/B07L7TRJX3/

17. https://www.amazon.com/Stray-Covenant-paranormal-romance-werewolf-ebook/dp/B07N49SCXT/

18. https://www.amazon.com/Rocks-Stones-Between-Rose-reverse-ebook/dp/B07FHSSY2Z/

19. https://www.amazon.com/Rocks-Stones-Between-Rose-reverse-ebook/dp/B07F56QN87/

20. https://www.amazon.com/Pretty-Fin-Adult-Mermaid-Romance-ebook/dp/B0838JDM6L/

21. https://www.amazon.com/Pretty-Fin-Raging-Seas-Mermaid-ebook/dp/B08DHFP17H/

Please leave a <u>Review!</u>

Reviews help author's get their books noticed! Your opinion matters. I want to personally thank you. And on behalf of all Writers, I thank you for taking the time to share your thoughts on the book you read!

Smokey Moment

For information on use of this material or for help with indie publishing needs contact Smokey Moment.

Email us at: bookbabepublishing@gmail.com

Thank you!

Smokey Moment

Smokey Moment

Don't miss out!

Visit the website below and you can sign up to receive emails whenever Smokey Moment publishes a new book. There's no charge and no obligation.

https://books2read.com/r/B-A-ZVPL-GEOIB

BOOKS 2 READ

Connecting independent readers to independent writers.

Also by Smokey Moment

Her Sister's Husband